street
people

street
people
a novella

Michael Nava

Kórima Press

An earlier version of this story was published in Finale: Short Stories of Mystery and Suspense (Alyson Pub. 1989), ed. Michael Nava.

Front Cover Photography: Louis Jacinto
Back Cover Photography: Michael Nava

Author photograph: Louis Jacinto

Cover and Book Design: Lorenzo Herrera y Lozano

Published by Kórima Press
San Francisco, CA
www.korimapress.com

ISBN: 978-1-945521-03-4

for here there is no place
that does not see you. You must change your life.

> — Rainer Maria Rilke,
>   "Archaic Torso of Apollo"

street people

i.

On a warm night in May, 1988, as the sky above Los Angeles glowed Martian red, Ben Manso pushed his way into a 7-Eleven on Santa Monica Boulevard to buy cigarettes and condoms. The only other people in the store were a kid standing at the check-out counter and the clerk standing behind it. The boy was scrawny, brown-haired and dark-eyed—Mexican, Ben thought, wearing jeans, a dirty tee-shirt, and ratty sneakers. Waiting his turn behind the kid, Ben watched him carefully place his purchases on the grubby formica counter: a bag of Doritos, two pre-wrapped ham and cheese sandwiches, a carton of milk, and a Hostess cupcake.

The clerk's nametag identified him as Ahmed. He rang up the boy's purchases, peered at him through thick glasses and said, "Five dollars and thirty-two cents."

The boy pulled a handful of crumpled bills and some change from his pants pocket and dumped them on the counter.

Patiently, Ahmed counted it. "This is only four-fifty," he said gently. "Not enough. You have to put something back."

The boy stared at him helplessly.

Ahmed picked up the cupcakes. "Take this back, ok?"

Mouth quivering, the kid took the pastry and lurched backwards, bumping into Ben.

"Sorry," he whispered.

"Wait a second," Ben said. "I'll pay for his food and give me a pack of Merits."

"Just the cigarettes?" the clerk asked.

"No," Ben said, "A pack of Trojans, too."

Ben slapped a twenty on the counter. Ahmed got the cigarettes and rubbers, rang everything up, and bagged the boy's groceries. The boy grabbed the bag and threw Ben a look of startled gratitude as he hurried out of the store.

"Kind of late to be grocery shopping," Ben said.

"He's a street kid," Ahmed replied. "He eats when he's got the money. You need matches?"

"Thanks," Ben said, accepting a matchbook advertising a nearby bailbondsman. "Are you saying he hustles?"

"Could be," Ahmed said.

"He can't be more than eight or nine."

Ahmed shrugged. "If he's a seller, there's a buyer."

Ben tucked the cigarettes and matchbook into the pocket of his unlined ash-gray silk blazer. "You must see a lot of sick shit working here."

Ahmed laughed. "Yeah, they don't call it the graveyard shift for nothing." He picked up the rubbers. "Don't forget these. Someone's getting lucky."

Ben shrugged. "Business."

"Ah," Ahmed said. "Take care my friend."

Out in the parking lot, one of his pagers went off. He spotted a phone booth at the corner. Heavy traffic moved in both directions on the boulevard and the air was foul with exhaust fumes. Across the street, a teen-age kid with a mop of wild hair, in tight jeans and a

wife-beater, stood beneath a streetlight smoking
and peering at the passing cars. Ben stepped
into the phone booth, pulled the door shut, and
watched a blue Corolla pull up to the curb in
front of the teen. All Ben could see of the driver
was that he was male with salt-and-pepper hair,
wearing a blue Dodgers windbreaker. The boy
approached the car, leaned into the window and
after a brief exchange with the driver, opened
the passenger door and climbed inside.

"Hey, Pete," Ben said, watching the car's
tail lights merge into traffic.

"I got a guy who'll pay to watch us get it
on," Pete said. "You in?"

"I have a date tonight,," Ben said.

"Meredith get to you first?"

"Yeah, it's an overnight. Sorry, Petey."

"Okay, cool," he said. "Call me tomorrow."

"Yeah," Ben said.

He hung up. A panhandler emerged from
the darkness and leaned drunkenly against
Ben's Fiat. Ben smelled the guy before he
reached him; he reeked of booze, body odor
and unwashed clothing

"Hey, man," Ben said. "Do you mind?"

"This your car?" the man asked, carefully
forming each word.

The drunk pushed himself off the hood, pulled a filthy rag from his back pocket and said, "I'll clean the windshield for a buck."

"The windshield is fine," Ben said.

"Please, man, I really need a drink."

Impulsively, Ben asked, "What's your name?"

It took the drunk a minute to remember. "Ron."

Ben handed him a ten. "Here you go, Ron, for protecting my car."

"Hey, thanks," Ron said. "Thanks a lot."

Clutching the bill in his hand, he lurched into the store.

Driving down the boulevard, Ben saw the kid from the store on the other side of the street lugging his little sack of groceries. He was trying to look tough but when Ben honked at him and waved, the boy jumped. He stared after Ben as if he'd seen Santa Claus and waved wildly with his free hand. For a second, Ben thought about turning around and giving the kid a ride, but he was already running late and the boy was no longer visible in his rearview mirror anyway.

He turned off Franklin and headed up the hills into a neighborhood of twisting, narrow roads, and enormous houses that commanded expensive views of the city below. At a stop sign, he fluffed his hair, put out his cigarette, and popped a breath mint. The thick scent of tuberoses in the bouquet on the passenger's seat filled the air. Ellie was a regular, but even his regulars expected a little courtship before getting down to business: flowers to be admired and arranged in a fancy vase, the nice wine in the pretty glasses on the terrace, and the conversation that trailed off to the pregnant silence that was his signal to kiss her. No money changed hands—she had paid the agency when she requested him—but in the end, he was no different than the teen climbing into the Corolla to give a driver a ten buck blow job. They worked different streets, but they were both street people. He headed up the hill to her house.

Ben woke at dawn, grabbed his cigarettes, and made his way through the dark rooms of the hillside house to the terrace. A half-empty wine bottle and two glasses gathered dew on the patio table. He lit a cigarette and leaned over the railing. The air was cool, damp, and fragrant. There was movement in the thick brush below the deck and then a doe stepped forward.

"Hello," he whispered.

The deer lifted its head, met his eyes, and then plunged back into the brush. Ben thought back dreamily to a morning long ago, at one of the prep schools where he'd spent his childhood, awakening to the first snow and a family of deer huddled beneath shaggy branches of pine. Just as he had then, he wished he had someone to show this to. He remembered the boy from the 7-Eleven. He would have liked the boy to have seen this; to have seen something beautiful.

Wade was outside his apartment in his walker when Ben let himself into the building. The old man smiled, or grimaced, it was hard to tell which. Since he'd broken his hip the summer before he was always more or less in pain. He was shapeless in an oversized, ragged Pendleton shirt and pair of baggy khakis. His mottled skin was like the fly-specked pages of an old book and time had dissolved his features into a puddle topped by a crown of wispy white hair. His blue eyes were still bright, however, and they missed nothing.

"Just getting home, baby?" he wheezed.

"Yeah."

"You want some coffee?"

"Sure."

"Come on in and put on a pot," Wade said.

Unless he was sleeping, Wade kept his front door open. He spent most of the day in a rocker that faced the door, trying to snare passersby into his room to visit. The other tenants hurried by because once Wade got started it was hard to shut him up. Ben didn't mind. Ben was as natural a listener as Wade was a talker. He liked to hear the old man's stories of his days as a bit player at the studios, tales documented by the black-and-white photographs that lined the walls of his apartment showing him with the big stars of the forties and fifties.

Wade's room smelled faintly of bird shit. He had had a pair of canaries, Goneril and Regan. Opening the cage door to change the water one day, he'd moved too slowly and the birds had flown out and through an open window. Wade had refused Ben's offer to replace the birds telling him, "At this rate, they'd outlive me, then what would happen to them? Unless you'd take care them."

Ben shrugged, "I don't know, Wade. Birds in cages? Might creep out some of my johns."

"I thought you were strictly out-call," Wade crackled.

Ben smiled, "I make exceptions for the right amount of money."

Wade knew Ben was a hustler but made no judgments since, as he had told Ben more than once, "Everyone in Hollywood has a price."

Ben worked for an agency called White Knights, which provided escorts to women, but also free-lanced on the side with men. White Knights was operated by a woman named Meredith, whom he had met through Pete when they were cater waiters for the same company. One night, after working a party at Bel-Air in a steel-and-concrete house that reminded Ben of an airport hanger, he'd gone home with Pete. Later, lying in bed, Pete told him, "You're good at sex."

"Thanks, I guess."

"No, I mean it," he said, taking a drag from Ben's cigarette. "Most guys are lousy at it because all they care about is getting off. You pay attention to the other person." He took another puff. "You fuck women, too?"

"You wanna do a threesome?"

"Just answer the question, man."

He shrugged. "I've had sex with women."

"Would you fuck someone for money?"

"You mean would I whore myself out?" Ben asked.

"Yeah, could you do it for money?"

"I never thought about it," Ben said.

"Think about it now."

Ben stubbed out his cigarette. For the most part, Ben, being naturally accommodating, had sex with people because they wanted him and because, having little sexual passion of his own, it interested him to observe theirs. Reading in bed late into the night was more thrilling for him than sex, a legacy of his years of boarding school when, after lights out, he had read secretly by flashlight beneath the covers in the narrow, uncomfortable beds that seemed to furnish every dorm room he had ever occupied.

"Sure," he told Pete. "Why not?"

Pete grinned and said, "There's someone I want you to meet."

"What are you?" Meredith had asked Ben during his interview.

"I beg your pardon, ma'am?"

"Ah," she said, approvingly, "nice manners, but drop the ma'am. It makes women feel old. Your look," she continued. "It's All-American boy, but there's something about your eyes and skin that's rather...exotic."

She studied him with the intensity of a jeweler examining a diamond for weight, flaws, and luminosity. Her large office, on a side street off Rodeo Drive was aggressively feminine down to the spindly white and gilt Louis XIV chair on which Ben perched. Meredith herself was a tiny woman who favored shoulder pads, wore her short blonde hair like a lacquered helmet, and exuded the faint rose scent of Jean Patou's "Joy." Heavy but expertly applied make-up concealed any vestige of personality, but even it could not hide her square, determined jaw and shrewd eyes. Later he would learn Meredith ran the business with her lover, Carol, who, apart from being a brunette, could have been Meredith's twin.

"Your last name, Manso," she said, speculatively. "Italian?"

"Spanish," Ben told her. "My father was Mexican-American, my mom is white."

"Ah," she said. "That explains it. God, you mixed race boys are gorgeous. Pete says you're bisexual."

"I guess," he said. "I've never thought about it much."

"I don't care what you are," she continued briskly, "as long as you can perform with a woman. Can you?"

"Yes," he said, biting off the 'ma'am.' "I've been with women."

"Of course," she said quickly, "White Knights is in the business of providing companionship, not sex. Still, what happens between you and the client once she's paid for your time is entirely up to her. Do you understand, Ben?"

He nodded.

"Oh," she said, "and you can sleep with boys on your own time, if that's what you're into, but use protection and I'd better not find out you're hustling men on the side. I will cut your balls off if I catch you free lancing." She extracted a business card from her desk drawer and slid it to him. "This is our photographer. Make an appointment with him for this week. He's very good, the best. Of course, you're giving him a lot to work with."

He tucked the card into his coat pocket. "What do you do with the pictures?"

"They go into the book," she said.

"The book?"

"The one our clients look through when they come in for an escort."

"What kind of pictures?" he asked, nervously.

She smiled, "Don't worry, Ben. They're headshots and one or two with your shirt off. Nothing that would embarrass your mother."

Ben helped Wade into his rocker.

"God, being old is fucked," Wade said. "It's the most depressing thing in the world."

Ben smiled. "Yesterday you said bad drag was the most depressing thing in the world."

"This is worse." Wade rocked morosely.

From the doorway of the little kitchen, Ben asked, "Did you eat today?"

"Yeah, yeah."

Inside the refrigerator was a can of Folgers, a few slices of bologna, half a loaf of bread, assorted condiments, and something in a Tupperware container covered with fuzzy mold.

"Make a grocery list. I'll go shopping for you," Ben said and set about making coffee.

"So, what was it last night," Wade asked when Ben brought him a mug of coffee. "Scrumptious dick or disgusting cooze?"

Ben sat on the floor, back against Wade's narrow bed, and smiled. "A woman."

Wade pretended to shudder.

"Your doctor's a woman. You like her."

"I've loved many women in my time," Wade replied. "From the neck up." He blew across the surface of his coffee. "You ever fall in love with any of your tricks?"

"You know the old saying, Wade, when you start to come with your johns it's time to get out of the business."

Wade cackled. "You're pretty smart for a whore."

"No, I'm just another pretty face."

"That you are, my boy. You prefer tricking with men or women?"

"Money doesn't have a gender."

"*Get* her."

Restlessly, Ben's gaze swept across the room. Over a dusty desk was a framed photograph of the young Wade standing at the gates of MGM with a teen-aged Judy Garland.

He remembered asking Wade, "What was she like?"

"Fifteen going on fifty, poor thing," Wade had replied.

He told Wade about the kid he'd seen at the store the night before.

"He couldn't have been more than eight. The guy at the 7-Eleven thinks he hustles."

"The queen who used to manage this place let street kids stay here. I think he took the rent in trade. Filthy little things."

"Not this one," Ben said. "He was just a little boy. Too young to be out on the streets."

"Life's a bitch, and then you die."

"You've been reading too many tee-shirts," Ben replied. "What do you want from the store?"

After he'd stocked Wade's refrigerator, he went up to his own apartment. It was one of the few one bedrooms in the building otherwise consisting of studios. The three-story complex was constructed around an interior courtyard dominated by a swimming pool where the tenants—most of them gay men—could be found lounging like 1950's starlets in the briefest swimsuits the management allowed. Sometimes, late at night, the murmurs and grunts of sex drifted up to his second floor window from boys playing in the hot tub. Another night, two guys, fighting loudly, stumbled drunkenly into the courtyard, one of them screaming, "Why won't you fuck me anymore! You never fuck me anymore!" Another tenant shouted from the third floor, "I'll fuck you if it'll shut you up!" Ben spent time at the pool tanning and swimming laps to stay in shape for work, but deflected all come ons from his neighbors to Wade's amazement.

"You said no to *him*?" Wade asked incredulously when the hot blond in apartment 231 passed them in the hall with a disappointed pout. "Why?"

"I didn't feel like it," Ben replied.

"Honey, are you sure you're gay?" Wade asked and, when Ben failed to respond, continued. "Don't tell me you're straight."

"I'm not anything but me," Ben said, putting an end to an uncomfortable conversation because, while he knew the old man would have cackled tolerantly over any form of sexual deviance, even his tolerance might have been tested had Ben told him the truth: except as work, sex rarely interested him. When he did feel the itch, he hooked up with Pete.

Ben's apartment had come furnished with a dowdy living room suite to which he had added a desk, a coffee table, an expensive entertainment center with a stereo he rarely used and a television he rarely watched. Two stolid bookcases were crammed with the books that were his entertainment of choice. He read vociferously and indiscriminately, pulling whatever seemed interesting from the shelves of the bookstore at the end of the street. He'd picked up the reading habit in boarding school, where books were his escape from the taunts and come ons of the other boys. They, it seemed, had known before he did there was something different about him. He had been a beautiful little boy and, skipping the awkward stage of pimples and ungainliness, his good looks had only deepened when he reached puberty, attracting both bullies and would-be seducers in the all-male schools. Sometimes it was the same boy, red-faced and panting, who, pinning Ben against a wall, stared at him in helpless confusion as if he couldn't decide whether to punch Ben or kiss him. Ben feared the first and rebuffed the second. All he wanted was to be left alone.

There were no pictures on the white walls of Ben's apartment, only a photograph on a side table. The photograph was of of his mother, father, and seven-year-old Ben, taken in Santa Monica the year his father died. He lit a cigarette, dialed Pete's number and picked up the photograph. They were pictured in front of their house which, he remembered, was painted deep blue and had a palm tree in the front yard. His mother wore a simple cotton dress and a breeze lifted her hair, his father was in a dress shirt and dark trousers, and Ben, standing between them, wore shorts and a Hawaiian shirt decorated with parrots. He was smiling. They all were.

"Yeah, it's Pete."

"Hey, Petey," Ben said. "You find someone for your gig last night."

"Yeah, Brady."

"From the agency? I thought he was straight."

Pete sucked in air and when he spoke he was holding his breath. "He is, and he fucked like a straight guy too, jack rabbiting me like he couldn't wait to get it over with. My ass is still sore."

"You getting high?"

"Yeah," he said, exhaling. "Why don't you come over."

"Gotta work tonight," he said.

"What, Meredith got you another date?"

"No. Cater waiter."

Pete laughed. "Fuck, Ben, you must be making money hand over fist hustling. Why are you still working catering gigs?"

"Sometimes I need to work a job where I get to keep my pants on."

"But you look so good with them off," Pete said, laughing.

"I'll call you when I get off work. We'll hang out."

"Later, dude," Pete said, wheezing as he inhaled.

The beginning of summer brought the marine layer and June gloom to the city. Ben, awakening to yet another morning of gray skies, headed out to Venice where he sunned himself on the gay beach and split a joint with a surfer dude who he then let blow him in a toilet stall. As he headed down the boardwalk to his car, a big hand clamped his shoulder. Ben shook it off and spun around. The guy who'd grabbed him wore a black tank-top and cut-off jeans that revealed a pale, bloated body. There was something vaguely familiar about the man's bleary face.

"You remember me?" he asked hopefully.

Ben peered at him. It was the drunk Ben had given money to outside the 7-Eleven.

"Sure," Ben said. "Ray? No, Ron, right?"

Ron nodded. "I saw you and wanted to say hi."

"You get around."

"The beach is free," he said, hostility creeping into his voice. Catching himself, he smiled nervously and added, "I take the bus."

"Yeah, well, it's a beautiful day. Enjoy," Ben said, moving away.

"The thing is," Ron said, "I need bus fare back into town. Could you maybe help me out?"

Ben stopped, pulled his wallet out his trunks and opened it. "Will a couple of bucks do it?"

Ron grabbed the wallet out of his hand and started running down the crowded boardwalk.

"Fuck," Ben said, stunned for a moment. He started after him but Ron ducked down one of the alleys off the boardwalk. By the time Ben reached it, the man was gone. Ben stopped to catch his breath. He looked around for the police who patrolled the boardwalk in walking shorts and black patent leather shoes. Seeing none, he stood irresolutely for a moment and then headed to his car, grateful he still had his keys. At the Venice substation, a harried cop took a report from Ben between phone calls. He didn't offer Ben much hope of recovering the wallet. Ben spent the rest of the day obtaining a new driver's license and cancelling credit cards.

Ben stopped in at Wade's on his way to the laundromat to pick up a bag of Wade's dirty clothes. He found the old man in his rocker looking at the back pages of one the gay rags where escorts advertised their services.

"This is you, isn't it?" Wade asked, tapping a picture of a headless, naked torso.

Ben looked over his shoulder. "How did you know?"

"The mole beneath your right nipple," he said. " 'Scotty. All-American boy, six feet, one hundred and eighty pounds, top, providing the boyfriend experience.' "

"How do you know about my mole?" Ben asked, grabbing Wade's laundry bag off the floor.

"Honey, when I'm not sitting by the door, I sit by the window and watch you boys sunning yourselves at the pool. Oh, don't make that face. With all the pills I take, I couldn't get it up if Keanu Reeves walked in the door buck naked, but I still like to look."

"I wasn't making that face at you," Ben said. "But, if you recognize my body, maybe other people might."

"That ball-busting madam you work for? Do you really think she scours the back pages of the gay rags to check on her boys?"

"I wouldn't put it past her," he said.

"You ever sleep with anyone who's not paying you?" Wade asked.

"Pete," Ben replied.

Wade smirked. "Not that public utility. A lover."

"The only person I ever loved was my dad," Ben said, "and he died."

Wade looked at him tenderly and said, "He didn't do it to hurt you, baby."

Ben held out the canvas bag stuffed with Wade's laundry and asked, "This everything?"

The regulars at the West Hollywood Wash 'n Dry were either Mexican women or gay men. The women brought their laundry in pillow cases and grocery bags carried in from big rusted-out cars. The gay men came in carting wicker baskets and paperback novels and cruised each other listlessly beneath the buzzing lights. The two groups could have been on different planets for all the contact between them.

Sitting in his car, Ben smoked a joint and listened to Tracy Chapman while he waited for his clothes to finish washing. He had a nice buzz on, mellow and benign, and he wondered, as he watched the weary women and the mannered men, what he added up to, being half of each. Half-Mexican, for sure. Half gay? He slept with women for money but recreationally only with men. So maybe he was more than half gay, but then again, except for sex, what did he really have in common with the skinny men in tight clothes and ruthlessly styled hair folding their laundry with prissy precision?

Pete was right, Ben was good at sex. He had learned early on to read the signs for what his partners wanted, whether it was in their eyes or in their grips or how they moved beneath or atop him. Most people, he had discovered, did not know how to ask for what they wanted in bed but wanted desperately to be given it. He obliged them since what they wanted was either to dominate or to be dominated. Those, rather than straight or gay, were the real categories of sexual orientation; the gender of the bodies was incidental. Ben could be either submissive or dominant, it was all the same to him. Sex was either work or an occasional distraction, but not an identity. What he wanted had nothing to do with sex. What he wanted was to belong but that had only happened once, and briefly, when he was a little boy standing beside his father in a shirt decorated with parrots.

One of the Mexican women stuffing clothes into a washer reminded him of his grandmother, his father's mother, whom he had not seen since his father's funeral. He remembered her as a dumpling of a woman, her white hair a crown of braided coils atop her head, her life mapped out in the deep lines and wrinkles on her face, her English awkward and heavily accented. She lived in a shabby house in a run-down neighborhood with a big yard and an apple tree; she would boost him into the tree to toss apples to her that she baked into pies with crusts the chewy texture of tortillas. He still dreamed of her. When he had first returned to Los Angeles to make a last stab at college, he called his mother and asked

for his grandmother's address. She told him she
had lost touch with the Mansos.

"I don't really remember anything about
those people, Ben," she said. She was in
in Chicago, her hometown, where she had
returned with him to her family after his
father's death.

" 'Those people,' mom'? They're dad's
family. My family."

"Don't be ridiculous, Benjamin," she
replied. He heard the clink of ice as she raised
her glass to her lips. "Your family's here."

The memory of that conversation triggered
a chain of associations involving his treatment
by his mother's family that threatened to
spoil his high. Her high WASP parents had
disapproved of her marriage to the Mexican-
American medical student she had met in her
last year at UCLA; so much so that they had
never laid eyes on Ben until she had returned
to the family fold, bringing her green-eyed,
olive-skinned, black haired child with her.
While she was welcomed back, he remained
a reminder of her indiscretion and a literal
black sheep in a family of pale, flinty-eyed
blonds. His grandfather joshingly called Ben
"Mutt," a name gradually adopted by everyone

in the family. When he was ten, his mother married a country club suitor who decided Ben should attend a boarding school, the first of several where he would pass his adolescence. Each time he returned home, for Christmas or summer break, Ben confronted a woman who seemed younger, thinner, and blonder than before, until it hardly seemed possible to him that she was his mother. It had been a mere formality when, after he dropped out of Cal State L.A., the last of four colleges he attended, she cut him off in a show of what she referred to, ice clinking in her glass on her end of the call, as "tough love." By then he had long since decided she bore him no love, tough or otherwise, and while the halting of his allowance was painful, her disappearance from his life was not.

Your family's here. He cranked up the music and took a deep hit off the joint to smother the resentment that clouded his chest. Once, when he was drunk, Ben went looking for the house he'd lived in as a child. A black family had bought it. They'd sobered him up and let him have his cry, then sent him on his way. Now, when anyone asked him, and he had to provide an answer, he said he was an orphan.

"*You got a fast car...*" A siren's wail broke through Tracy Chapman's voice. On the street an ambulance was stuck in traffic, lights flashing, siren blaring. His father had been killed in a car wreck, driving home late from the hospital where he was finishing up his residency. Of that terrible night, Ben remembered only being awakened by his mother's sobs in the early morning hours and wandering out of his bedroom in his pajamas where he found her collapsed on the couch with a police officer standing over her. He had never been awake past nine and it had seemed to him that he had entered another planet, cold and gray, where the familiar shapes of the furniture were distorted and frightening and his mother's grief-stricken eyes were like caverns. Ben never saw his father again—the funeral was closed coffin and, in any event, he became so hysterical his grandmother ushered him out of the church half-way through the service. Sometimes it seemed to him he had never left the chilly, colorless planet where his childhood had ended.

Ben sucked at the joint until the pot gradually infiltrated his brain and calmed him down again. He glanced at his watch. His wash would be about done. He stepped into the humid laundromat and spotted an empty dryer at the far end of the room. Piling his clothes into a cart, he headed toward it. Just before he got there a boy stepped out, his back to Ben, and opened the dryer door.

"Hey, you gonna use that dryer?" Ben asked.

The boy spun around. It was the kid he'd seen at the 7-Eleven. Without a word, the boy slipped away to a tall, thin man folding pillow cases at the end of a long table nearby. The man was grizzled, stooped, and nearly bald. He wore a cheap plaid shirt, black 501s, and orange construction boots. The boy looked at Ben, who smiled. The boy smiled back for a second, then backed up, brushing against the man's legs.

Sourly, the man looked down at the boy and then up at Ben. Smiling resolutely, Ben approached them.

"Hi," he said. "I asked your friend here if he needed that dryer."

"No, we're finished," the man said. "He was just making sure he got everything out of it."

He went back to his folding.

"Your son?"

"That's right." His eyes were bleary and suspicious. Something about him hit a note that wasn't close to paternal.

"We met before," Ben said to the man, and then to the boy. "Remember? Back in May, at the 7-Eleven."

The boy slowly nodded, recognition flooding his eyes.

"My name's Ben."

"Frank," the man said. "And Bobby."

"Hi," Ben said to Bobby.

Bobby whispered, "Hi."

"How old are you, eight, nine?"

"He's eight," Frank said.

"I'm eight-and-a-half," Bobby said huskily.

"I guess that six months means a lot when you're eight," Ben said. "When's your birthday?"

"In six months," Frank said abruptly. "That's his birthday. If you want that dryer, you better hustle."

A big woman carrying a basket of sopping clothes waddled toward the dryer where Ben had left his cart. He hurried over and stuffed his clothes into the machine. She grunted and turned away. He put a couple of quarters into the dryer and pushed in the slot. Nothing happened.

"Shit," he said, turning back toward Frank and Bobby. "Was this thing working when you...? " The man and the boy were gone.

When he finished his wash, Ben drove back to the 7-Eleven where he'd first seen Bobby. He'd returned to the store after he was robbed to ask Ahmed if he knew anything about Ron, but Ahmed couldn't help him. Now he occasionally stopped when he was in the neighborhood to shoot the breeze with the clerk. The door buzzer yelped as he stepped inside. Ahmed looked up from his *Playgirl* and smiled.

"My friend," he said. "Pack of Merits?"

"Yeah, thanks," Ben said, taking the cigarettes. He opened the pack, offered one to Ahmed and observed, "Business is slow."

Ahmed lit their cigarettes. "It's early," he said with a thin smile. "The boys have to turn their first tricks before they can buy anything."

"Do you remember that little kid who was here the first time I came in?"

"Yes," Ahmed said agreeably.

Ben exhaled a stream of smoke. "No you don't."

Ahmed shrugged. "There are so many." He narrowed his eyes. "The little Mexican boy," he said finally. "You paid for his food."

"That's the one. Have you ever seen him in here with a guy named Frank?"

"I haven't seen him for a long time," Ahmed replied, "and when he came in he was always alone. He put his dirty dollar bills on the counter." He touched the counter with a long finger. "Sometimes they were enough, sometimes not. You helped him that time, maybe this man is helping him now."

"I know a john when I see one," Ben said.

"Everyone is someone's john on this street."

"The kid is only eight years old. That should shock even you."

"Did he look healthy?" Ahmed asked. "Well fed? Did he have shoes?" Ahmed crushed his cigarette in a green foil ashtray. "Sex is all these kids have to bargain with. They're lucky someone wants them." He tapped the magazine. "Me, I prefer Mr. September Or you, if I could afford you."

"You've been at this job too long, Ahmed. How much are the smokes?"

"On the house."

"I'll see you around," Ben said, starting out the door.

"Ben."

He turned. "What?"

"Stick around. I'll show you ten kids who need your help more than your little friend does."

"You sure you don't want some of this?"

"Yeah, I'm sure."

Pete expertly cut another line of coke on the *Thriller* jewel case, snorted it and sagged against Ben. The plantation shutters were drawn against the sun—it was almost three—casting Pete's bedroom into a twilight illuminated only by a dim bedside lamp and a crack of light escaping from the half-opened bathroom door. The thick air smelled of poppers, sweat, and cum. A Peter Gabriel CD repeated on the boom box on the dresser. The mirrored closet doors reflected the two naked men in the tangle of sheets on Pete's king size water bed.

Sinewy, smooth-skinned, and sandy haired, Pete looked like the cute grocery store check-out boy you over tipped for carrying your bags to your car. His sweet good looks disguised, as Ben had discovered, a personality devoted entirely to the pursuit of pleasure, mostly in the form of sex and drugs, but he was so good-natured he was impossible to dislike, even as he regaled Ben with his tales of debauchery. He had told Ben that many of his male tricks liked to have him pretend he was their son, especially the married guys who actually had sons.

"Half of them want me to say, harder daddy, when they're fucking me," he told Ben, "and the other half want me to say, no, daddy, stop, it hurts."

"That's kind of twisted," Ben said.

Pete laughed, "Which one? It's fantasy, Benny. They fuck me and their sons are safe, so it's like I'm doing a public service. Like you, clearing out the cobwebs in the pussies of those rich housewives after their husbands have dumped them for a newer model. We deserve medals!"

It was also Pete who, when Ben had expressed doubts before going on his first escort date for Meredith, told him, "You'll be fine, Benny. You're a giver."

"A giver?"

"Yeah, dude. The world's divided between givers and takers. Givers take care of people, takers get taken care of."

"What are you?"

Pete smirked. "Taker."

And it was Pete who had convinced Ben to branch out to men when one of his regulars had requested another guy. He told Ben most of Meredith's boys moonlighted because men hired more often and paid more, "plus," he reminded him, "there's no pimp taking her cut." He had made it sound like he was doing Ben a favor.

He grabbed Ben's limp cock and said, "Get it up, Benny, I need your pretty cock in me like now."

"We're out of rubbers," Ben said.

"Don't need rubbers," Pete said, stroking Ben.

Ben pulled away. "Are you crazy? Remember AIDS."

"Come on, dude. I let guys fuck me all the time without rubbers."

Ben stared at him. "You're joking."

"Nah. I charge them an extra hundred." He grinned. "Dude, look at us. We're not gonna get AIDS. AIDS is for those freaky Silverlake leather queens. Come on, Benny fuck me."

"Not doing it."

"Pussy. Let me at least suck you off while I got this buzz on."

"Yeah, sure."

Afterwards, Ben said, "Do you get tested?"

Pete shrugged. "Huh? Oh, that. Nah. I know I'm clean. Do you?"

"Yeah," Ben said. "I'm negative and I'm going to stay that way."

"You are such a fucking boy scout," Pete said. He chopped a fat line of coke. Before he snorted it, he said, "This one's for you, Benjamin."

When Peter Gabriel's "Sledgehammer" came on, Pete hopped out of bed, cranked up the volume on the boom box and began to dance, swinging his dick at Ben. He threw his hands above his head, gyrated his hips, spun around and pushed his ass out. He turned, eyes closed, singing loudly and off-key and then, abruptly, grabbed his chest and staggered forward. He collapsed in convulsions on the bed, creating a small tsunami on the water bed.

It was past midnight before Pete was stabilized and Ben left the hospital. On his way out, the ER doc stopped him and said, "Good thing you called 911 instead of leaving him there to die like most cokeheads."

"I'm not a cokehead."

"Whatever. You saved his life. Until the next time he overdoses."

He drove home with his windows down. June gloom had given way to a heat wave that had started around the Fourth of July and showed no signs of letting up. Half the city smelled like a fast-food dumpster, the other half reeked of jasmine. Ben pulled into his parking space in the underground garage, got out the car, and threw up. It was almost noon when he woke up with a grinding headache. He heard the tail end of a male voice leaving a message on the answering machine but could not make out the words. He pulled himself out of bed and stumbled into the bathroom where he drank tap water from cupped hands and swallowed aspirin and a valium. He called the hospital to check on Pete and then listened to the message on his answering machine from a police detective named Gomez asking him to call the Venice substation. Ben figured the hospital had alerted the cops to Pete's overdose and they wanted to question him about the coke. He considered ignoring the message but if the cops had his phone number, they could also get his address and come pounding at his door. He picked up the phone and dialed the number.

After he identified himself to the cop, Gomez said, "Yeah, Mr. Manso, you reported being robbed on the boardwalk last month, right?"

"Yes," Ben said. "Why, did you find my wallet?"

Gomez responded with a clipped, "We did."

"Where was it?" Ben asked, burrowing into the blankets as the valium kicked in.

"The guy still had it on him," Gomez replied.

"Is he in jail?" Ben asked through a yawn.

"He's dead, Mr. Manso."

Ben sat up. "You're kidding. Where?"

"They found him in an alley behind the boardwalk."

"Are you sure it's the same guy?"

"No, we're not. The only I.D. he had was your wallet and there wasn't much left in that but an address book and a couple of credit card receipts. I'd like you to come down and take a look at him."

Ben shivered. "You want me to what?"

"Take a look at him. If it's the same guy who stole your wallet that gives us something to work with in identifying him."

"You want me look at the body?"

"Look, Mr. Manso," he heard papers rustling. "Uh, Ben, look, this is a lot more serious than a stolen wallet now. Three street people have been killed in Venice this month alone. I need your help to find the killer."

"I just woke up," Ben muttered, as if this would excuse him.

"I'll be here 'til five," he said, in a tone that said he wouldn't be taking no for an answer.

"Okay," Ben said, grudgingly. "Give me an hour."

Gomez's first name was Ed. He was a big man, half a head taller than Ben, who was nearly six feet, and twenty pounds of muscle heavier. He had a stony, Latino handsomeness and scoured Ben with a look that made him wish he hadn't popped another valium in the car. Wasting no time on chit-chat, Gomez led Ben to one of the holding cells at the back of the police station. A green, plastic body bag lay on one of the two bunks.

"It's a good thing I caught you," Gomez said, conversationally. "He's going downtown to the coroner in about an hour."

"For what?"

"Autopsy," Gomez said. "You ready?" Without waiting for an answer, he unzipped the body bag, filling the room with the man's stench. "This the guy who robbed you?"

Ben looked quickly. Ron was wearing the same black tank-top he'd had on when he accosted Ben. The side of his head had been smashed in.

"Yeah," Ben gasped.

"Take another look," Gomez said, patiently. "I need you to be sure."

Ben looked again at the bloated, ash-colored face, the bloody hair.

"That's him. I'm sure. He said his name was Ron." He looked at Gomez. "I'm going to be sick."

"There's a toilet behind you."

Ben staggered to the metal toilet and threw up.

Back at Gomez's desk, the cop took Ben's statement and apologized for not being able to release his wallet.

Holding a big Styrofoam container of coffee between shaky hands, Ben said, "What about my address book? Can I have that?"

"Not today. I'll release it as soon as I can," Gomez said.

Ben wasn't up to arguing the point. He sipped his coffee. "Who'd want to kill a guy like that? He was just a drunk."

Gomez said, "He was an easy target, like most street people. They're drunks or addicts or have psych issues. They can't defend themselves."

"But why kill him? "

"You read about those high school kids in San Diego who set fire to a homeless guy for kicks? This was probably a thrill kill,too. Like I said on the phone, he's the third victim this month. We may have a serial killer out there targeting the homeless. What I worry about are the women and kids living on the streets."

Ben thought of Bobby. "Can I ask you about something?"

"Sure," Gomez said. He pulled a cigarette out of a pack of Winstons and lit it.

"There's a street kid around where I live, he's around eight. The first time I saw him he was alone. Then I saw him with this old guy who said he was the kid's father. I know he wasn't the kid's father. I think he picked the kid up off the street and he's abusing him. You know what I mean?"

"What makes you think that, Ben?"

"This friend of mine used to see the kid around and he was always by himself. Now, suddenly he's got a daddy. I saw them together and it didn't look right."

Gomez tapped ash into his trash can. "There's not much we can do about things that don't look right."

"The guy's molesting the kid."

"You don't know that," Gomez replied. "We don't investigate suspicions around here. We're busy enough with real crimes."

"Well, isn't it at least kidnapping?"

"Come on, Ben."

"What if I found out more?"

Gomez shook his head. "You don't want to be getting into other people's business."

"What about you? You're a cop. Don't you care that some pervert is hurting a little boy?"

Gomez dropped his cigarette to the floor and crushed it with the toe of a scuffed shoe. "You're upset, Ben," he said, coolly. "So I'll ignore that. Go home. Get some rest."

Ben got up. "Thanks for the coffee," he said, bitterly.

"I'll be in touch," Gomez replied, turning his attention to the pile of papers on his desk.

"The temperatures continue to be unseasonably warm as we head into August..."

Ben switched off the radio and rolled down his window; a blast of hot, gritty air swept into the car. The night sky was empty but for a sliver of moon. Approaching the intersection of Santa Monica and Fairfax, traffic came to a dead stop. Peering ahead, he saw that there'd been an accident. Flares were out, roadblocks were up, and a cop was directing traffic around a stopped car, crushed motorcycle and a sheeted body. Ben wheeled into the parking lot of a fast food drive-in looking for an exit onto Fairfax. As he swung behind the building, he heard a racket near the dumpster. A kid was trying to climb the metal wall but couldn't get a foothold. He dropped down and stumbled to his knees. The kid glanced at him. It was Bobby. Ben pulled over and parked. He got out of the car and walked to the dumpster where the boy had balled himself into a frightened crouch.

"Hey, Bobby." Ben said. "It's okay. It's me, Ben. Do you remember me?"

The boy looked up and nodded.

"Where's Frank?" Ben asked.

"Sick," the boy whispered. His clothes were shabbier and dirtier than when Ben had last

seen him. He gave off a thin, rancid smell and
his hair was matted greasily to his skull.

Pointing to the dumpster, Ben asked,
"What were you doing in there?"

The boy began to cry. "I'm hungry."

"Come on," Ben said, taking him by the arm
and leading him toward his car.

The boy struggled weakly to get away.
"Frank said—"

"Forget about what Frank said," Ben
replied. "Let's get you something to eat."

The boy gave up and let Ben drag him into
his car.

In his apartment, Ben put together a meal
from the odds and ends of take-out in his
refrigerator. Bobby ate everything, his attention
riveted to the plate as if he were afraid to look
at Ben. When he finished eating, Ben brewed
him a cup of mint tea and sat down with him at
the table. The boy leaned back in his chair and
as far away from Ben as he could get.

"I'm not going to hurt you, Bobby."

"I should go home," he said, weakly.

"Where do you live?" Ben asked.

"8900 Sunset Boulevard. Room 221," he
recited.

"Is that where Frank is?"

Tears welled up in his eyes. "He stopped talking."

"Who, Frank?"

Bobby nodded, snot running down his nose. Ben handed him a paper napkin and told him to blow.

"I think he's dead," the boy sniffled.

"That's all right," Ben said, stupidly. "Finish your tea. You want to watch some TV?"

"Okay," Bobby said, and began to cry again.

The boy fell asleep in front of the TV and Ben carried him into his bed. Returning to the living room, he lit a cigarette and shut the TV off. It was a little before eleven. He thought about Frank and knew he should do something. He could call the cops, but then what would happen to Bobby? Instead, he went downstairs to Wade's apartment where Ben found the old man in a voluminous nightgown, sitting in his rocker like Whistler's mother and reading a biography of Elizabeth Taylor.

"Hello, honey," he said to Ben. "Early night?"

"I need you to do me a favor."

"That's why I'm here, baby."

"I need you to keep an eye on a kid in my apartment."

Wade cocked a shaggy eyebrow. "Kid? I hope he's legal, Ben."

"He's not a trick. It's the kid I told you about, the one I saw at 7-Eleven a couple of months back. I found him dumpster diving behind that hot dog place on Fairfax."

Quickly, he sketched the night's events for Wade.

"I don't mean to sound like Lily Law, honey, but isn't this a job for the police?"

Thinking bitterly of his conversation with Gomez two weeks earlier, he said, "The cops don't give a shit."

"He could be a runaway. His parents might be looking for him."

"What kind of parents let their eight-year-old run away from home?"

"You don't know how he ended up on the streets."

"Are you going to help or not?" Ben snapped.

"Where are you going?" Wade asked.

"Bobby gave me an address on Sunset where he said he and Frank are staying. I'm going to check on the guy."

"Okay, help me upstairs," Wade said, "but Ben this isn't a good idea."

The Sunset address was to a rundown motel at the end of the boulevard. A driveway dipped down from the street to a parking lot illuminated by a dim neon sign flashing the motel's name. Ben pulled into a space and got out of his car. From the edge of the lot was a panorama of the city from downtown to Century City, the lights scattered like confetti in the hot night. Ben made his way up to the second floor and down a long exposed hallway, past closed doors and the squall of TVs and radios and voices, to room 221. He knocked and when there was no response, pounded the door, cracking it open. He pushed his way in. The room was dark. He fumbled for a wall switch without success. Keeping the door open for light, he stepped inside but the stench forced him back out. Breathing through his mouth, he re-entered the room and stood still, accustoming his eyes to the darkness. He discerned a figure on an unmade bed.

"Frank?" he called, approaching the bed.

There was no response. He switched on the bedside lamp.

"Jesus."

Frank's bare body was skeletal and as gray as Ron's corpse had been. Beside the bed was a plastic bucket. Puke ran down its sides. Strewn nearby were empty hamburger containers from McDonald's. Frank's eyes were closed and his mouth hung open. Stumbling through the darkness, Ben hurried out of the room, slammed the door shut, and ran to his car. Back on Sunset, he saw a bar and skidded to a stop. Inside, he found a pay phone. Hands shaking, he dialed 911. The phone rang and rang.

"Answer the fucking phone," he said.

"Nine-one-one, what is your emergency?" a woman droned.

"I found a dead guy," he said, all in a rush. "He's in a motel room on Sunset. You got to send someone."

"Sir, sir," the woman interrupted. "Slow down."

"It's at 8900 Sunset, room 221," he said.

"Are you sure he's—"

"He's dead," Ben snapped. "Send someone."

"Sir, what's your name and where are you calling from?"

Ben hung up. He went into the bar and ordered a double bourbon. A few minutes later, he heard sirens passing on the street outside. When he went out to his car, he saw a black-and-white, red light flashing, turn into the motel driveway.

Wade's doctor, Iris Wong, was emerging from Ben's bedroom with her black bag in hand when Ben let himself into his apartment. Wade was sitting on the sofa, looking frail and exhausted.

"What happened?" Ben asked him.

Wade said, "He woke up, and wandered out here, delirious or something. When he saw me, he got hysterical. I didn't know what else to do, so I called Iris."

"Is he okay?" Ben asked her.

"He has a fever," she said coolly, "and it looks like he's suffering from malnutrition. Do you want to explain what's going on here, Ben?"

"You better sit down. It'll take a while."

She took a sharp breath, as if she were about to say something, but then sat. Ben had met her when he started driving Wade to his medical appointments. Over time, she started checking with him to make sure Wade's prescriptions were filled, that he was taking his medications and was eating something other than bags of Pepperidge Farms Milano cookies.

"Okay, Ben," she said. "I'm listening."

Ben told her the whole story.

When he finished, Iris said, "Excuse me," and disappeared into the bedroom, closing the door behind her. Fifteen minutes, later, she came out again and asked Ben, "Are you going to call the police, or should I?"

"What do you mean?" Ben asked.

"I'm a mandated reporter, Ben."

"A what?"

"State law requires physicians to report kids who they think have been abused to the police," she said. "It's a criminal offense if I don't."

"Can't you just forget you were here?"

She shook her head. "No, I can't. Who's going to take care of him, Ben?"

"I will."

"I know you mean well and I'm glad you keep an eye on Wade, but this is a very different situation. We're talking about a child. He has parents somewhere and he belongs with them." She stood up. "Give him baby aspirin and feed him something decent. And call the police."

"Does it have to be today? You said he's sick."

She frowned. "Fine, you can wait a day but I'll be checking up on you. Good-night."

After she left, Wade said, "I'm sorry, baby, but I couldn't handle him."

"That's okay, Wade. I'm glad she had a look at him."

He helped Wade to his apartment and then came back up and went into the bedroom. Bobby was a small lump beneath the blankets, his face upturned, eyes screwed shut, scowling. Ben sat at the edge of the bed and touched the boy's warm forehead. He stirred and muttered something.

Exhausted, Ben lay down beside him. Listening to the boy's noisy breathing, he fell asleep.

When Ben woke up, the digital clock read 3:11 and Bobby had climbed into his arms. The boy was weightless and stank of the streets. Ben had a sudden memory of himself as a child, standing tearfully at the edge of his parents' bed, driven into their room by a nightmare. His mother murmured, "Go back to bed, Benny." But his father had pulled back the covers and said, "Come here, *m'ijo*." He had clambered into their bed and his father had swept him against his chest; he remembered how his father's chest hairs had tickled his nose and the faint scent of his aftershave.

"I had a bad dream, *papi*," he told his father.

"I know, *m'ijo*, but you're safe here. I'll keep the bad dreams away."

Ben kissed the top of Bobby's head and slipped back into sleep.

When Iris Wong called him two days later, he lied and told her he had phoned the police and Bobby was gone, then he went downstairs to swear Wade to secrecy.

"Honey, what's your plan here?" Wade asked irritably. "He's not a stray puppy who followed you home. He's someone's child."

"I know that," Ben said. "When he's able to tell me what happened to him, I'll know what to do. For now, he's better off with me than on the streets or being passed around to strangers in foster care."

Wade regarded him shrewdly. "Is that what happened to you when you were a kid?"

"Close enough," he replied.

"You never talk about your childhood," Wade said.

"My dad died in a car crash when I was seven," he said, tersely. "We were living here in L.A. My mom took me back to Chicago where she was from. After she remarried, they sent me away, to school. I never lived with her again. With any of them. My family." He spat out the phrase.

"You had no one to take care of you," Wade observed.

"Whatever," Ben replied. "I took care of myself."

"You don't think Bobby can take care of himself?"

"Why should he?" Ben asked angrily. "Why should any kid?"

"Ok, honey," Wade said. "I'm not sure who you're trying to take care of here, but I won't say anything to Iris for now."

After the first few days, Ben decided that Bobby wasn't so much afraid of him as just generally afraid. He spoke—when he spoke—in a whisper, averted his eyes from Ben's, and seemed to curl into himself, taking up as little as space as possible. Ben responded with gentleness, not asking about Frank or anything that had happened to him. He bought Bobby toys and clothes and made him the food he remembered loving as a little boy—macaroni and cheese, fried chicken, spaghetti and tomato sauce. The boy accepted all this impassively. Then one day after finishing his grilled cheese sandwich and tomato soup lunch, Bobby said, "Can I have some chocolate ice cream?" It was the first time he'd ever asked for anything. After that, he seemed to unwind a bit, his voice a little stronger, his responses more than a word or two, and once or twice, he smiled at something Ben said. When he smiled, the fear left his eyes and he looked like a little boy. That, more than his terror, broke Ben's heart.

Ben, believing Bobby had been abused by Frank, had been careful not to touch the boy and, after the first night, had taken the couch and given Bobby his bed. But after a couple of nights, he was awakened by Bobby's whimpers and went into the bedroom where he found the boy twisting in the sheets and muttering. He perched at the edge of the bed and gently shook the boy's shoulders. Bobby awakened with a gasp.

"Were you having a nightmare?" Ben asked.

Bobby nodded.

"It's all right," Ben said. "Do you want something? A glass of water?"

"Can you stay here?" Bobby asked.

"Yeah." Ben said. He slipped into the bed. "Is this all right?"

"Yeah." Bobby murmured.

"Okay, *m'ijo*," Ben said. "Go back to sleep. I'll keep the bad dreams away." Ben, still worried that the proximity of his big male body might be disturbing to the boy after what he had been through with Frank, did not attempt to embrace Bobby but the boy climbed into his arms and clung to him like a life raft. Ben held the small body against his and listened to Bobby's breathing deepen trustingly into sleep. A sensation of tenderness surged through him, a primal protectiveness he had not felt before for anyone, and he knew that, as unprepared as he might be to take care of Bobby, he never wanted to let go of him.

The next morning, Ben sat down beside him as he ate his Cap'n Crunch and watched Bugs Bunny. "What are you watching?"

"Cartoons," he said softly. He spooned some cereal into his mouth. On the screen, Bugs appeared in drag on the back of a plump white horse.

"The night I brought you home with me I went to see Frank."

Without looking up at him, Bobby asked, "Can I have more juice?"

Ben took the boy's glass into the kitchen and filled it with apple juice. He handed it to the boy and watched the cartoon with him for a moment, before asking, "Bobby, did Frank hurt you?"

Eyes fastened to the screen, the boy shook his head.

"Look at me, Bobby," Ben said gently. Reluctantly, the boy looked at him. "Why were you staying with Frank?"

Bobby bowed his head and whispered, "Georgie told me to."

"Who's Georgie?"

The boy's breath got shallow. "Georgie's my brother."

Ben wondered if Georgie had been the boy's pimp or just another street kid who made some change by turning Bobby over to Frank. "Georgie gave you to Frank?"

The boy nodded.

"Bobby, where does your family live? Here in L.A.?"

"I can't tell you," Bobby said, distressed. "Georgie made me promise."

"Where is Georgie? Can I talk to him?"

"He's gone," he whispered. His eyes were fearful.

Ben backed off. "It's okay, Bobby. We can talk some more later. Just tell me, do you want to go home to your family?"

"Can I stay with you?" Bobby asked.

"Sure," Ben said.

When he called Meredith and told her he needed time off, she said, "We're in the service business, Ben. You have regulars. They depend on you."

"A vibrator could do what I do," he said.

"Is that supposed to be funny?" she asked, irritably.

"It's the truth," he said. "Anyway, I have a family thing I have to take care of."

"How much time are we talking about?"

"I don't know."

There was a long pause. "I'm sorry, Ben, I like you and you've been a good earner, but I can't cover for you indefinitely. I'm going to have to take you out of the book. Call me when you get your affairs straightened out and we'll talk."

Pete showed up at Ben's apartment unannounced after Ben told him he was out of the business.

"Who's the kid?" he asked after Ben sent Bobby to Wade's.

Ben told Pete how Bobby had come to stay with him.

"So what, you're going to adopt him?"

"I don't know what I'm going to do. Right now he's just staying here."

"You pick up some kid off the street and suddenly you're going straight? That's crazy, Benny."

Ben heard himself say, "I want a different life."

He waited for Pete's smart-ass rejoinder but Pete shrugged and said, "I always knew you were a closet square." He smiled. "It's been fun, Benny. Good luck with the kid."

"You should knock off the coke," Ben replied.

"I'm not like the kid," Pete replied. "I don't need a daddy unless he's rich and has an eight inch cock. Later, Ben."

When Ben thought about it later, it occurred to him that, without knowing it, he had been looking for a way out of escorting. It wasn't because being paid for sex felt degrading or immoral to him; it was no more than an undemanding job that required little of him except to show up, be pleasant, and have sex. He liked some of his clients and had developed something akin to friendship with a few of them. He could have drifted along for years, until he was too old or too jaded to continue, but then Bobby had come into his life. Ben had never had been responsible for anyone before Bobby so he had not realized that what he wanted, needed, was to matter to someone else. He remembered Wade's remark—*who are you taking care of here?*—and realized it was not only Bobby, but himself.

One afternoon, Ben returned from the supermarket with Bobby to find Iris Wong waiting outside his apartment.

"Hello, Bobby." she said pleasantly. "Ben, I'd like to talk to you for a moment. Privately."

"Wait here," he said. He and Bobby took the groceries into the apartment and he told Bobby to start putting them away. "I'll be right back."

He went back out into the hall, closing the door behind him.

"You lied to me," the doctor said. "You told me you had called the police."

"Did Wade tell you?" Ben asked bitterly.

"You left some of Bobby's toys in his apartment," she said. She shook her head irritably. "What do you think you're doing, Ben?"

"I'm taking care of a kid no one else cares about."

"He has a family, and you're not it. You could be charged with kidnapping."

"That's crazy," he said. "He got tossed out into the streets, sold to a child molester, and I'm the one who's breaking the law?"

"Has he actually told that's what happened?" she asked brusquely.

"I'm working on getting the story out of him," Ben said. "He's obviously been through a lot, and none of it was pretty."

In a softer tone, she said, "I don't doubt that but, Ben, you have absolutely no legal right to keep him with you. Do you understand that? You're breaking the law. There's no good Samaritan exception to child abduction. Not to mention the position you've put me in. I told you I was a mandated reporter, and the only reason I didn't call the police myself was because you said you would."

"I'm sorry," he mumbled. "I was trying to do what was best for him."

She sighed. "You'll call the police today or I will. Understand?"

"Please, Iris," he said. "Don't make me do that."

"I'll be back tomorrow. If he's still here, I will take him with me."

After she left, Ben considered his options. He knew she was serious about taking Bobby if he failed to call the police, but he worried about some strange cop showing up at his apartment and terrifying the boy. He thought about Detective Gomez. He had shrugged Ben off when Ben had first told him about Bobby, but maybe now that Ben had proof of his story, Gomez might be more sympathetic. He called the Venice police station.

"Hold the line please," he was told when he asked for Gomez.

From the kitchen table, Ben could hear Bobby quietly talking to himself in the living room. He craned his neck around the doorway. Bobby was playing with the Masters of the Universe dolls that Ben had bought the day before. He-Man was pounding Skeletor to a pulp while Bobby provided sound effects. He seemed just like a normal eight-year-old, Ben thought.

"This is Gomez."

"This is Ben Manso. You remember me? My wallet was stolen by the guy that got killed in Venice and I came down—"

"Yeah, sure, Ben. I'm afraid we can't release the wallet yet."

"That's not why I'm calling you," Ben said, lowering his voice. "Do you remember that I told you about the kid I'd seen on the streets?"

There was a dubious pause. "A kid on the streets?"

"Yeah. I told you he was being molested by a guy who said he was the kid's dad."

"Okay, I remember. What about it?"

"I found him going through the garbage behind a fast food place on Santa Monica. The guy who took him is dead."

When Gomez spoke again, his voice was alert and impersonal. "How do you know that?"

Ben explained how he'd gone to the motel.

"Where's the boy now?"

"Here," Ben said. "With me."

Gomez said, "I think you better come down here."

"I can't leave him alone."

"Bring him with you?"

"He'll freak out," Ben said. "Can't you come here?"

"What's the address?"

An hour later, Gomez was at his door. Ben let him in. Bobby stared at Gomez and then at his He-Man doll.

"Are you He-Man's brother?" he asked.

Gomez smiled briefly and shook his head.

"This is Detective Gomez," Ben said. "This is Bobby."

"Hi, Bobby."

To Ben, Gomez said, "Can we go somewhere private to talk?"

"The kitchen," Ben said. "You want a cup of coffee?"

Over coffee, Ben told Gomez everything, from his first meeting with Bobby to how Bobby was improving in Ben's care. The cop listened with the same cool attentiveness he'd shown the day Ben identified Ron's body in the drunk tank. When Ben finished, Gomez said, "You probably expect me to tell you what a good guy you are for taking the kid off the street, but the fact is, you should've done what that doctor told you and called me the day you found the kid."

"He was sick," Ben said.

"Child Services has doctors. The kid's already been traumatized on the streets and now I'm going to have to take him away from you and traumatize him all over again.

"He's happy here. No one else cares about him."

"His parents?"

"Where were his parents when that pedophile got his hands on him or when he was dumpster-diving for food?"

"I don't know," Gomez replied. "Maybe he ran away, maybe he was abducted. Maybe his parents are assholes or maybe they're sitting somewhere desperately hoping their son is still alive. The point is, he's got a family somewhere and he belongs to them."

"Why aren't they looking for him?"

"Do you know for a fact that they're not?"

It had not occurred to Ben that Bobby might have been abducted; he had assumed the boy was a runaway whom no one had wanted, except Ben.

"No," he said quietly.

"That's what I thought," Gomez said. "I'm going to have to take him with me."

Ben shook his head. "I won't let you."

The two men stared at each other. Finally, Gomez said, "What do you do for a living, Ben?"

"I work as a waiter for a catering company."

"No you don't," Gomez said quietly. He reached into his pocket and extracted the thin address book Ben carried in his wallet. "Remember this?" He opened it, flipping through the pages. "White Knights? I worked vice for a long time, Ben, I know about White Knights. You're a prostitute. Plus, you were stoned out of your mind the day you came down to the station. I bet I could walk into your bathroom and find enough of something to arrest you on the spot. Don't make me do that."

"I stopped escorting," Ben said, "and you're not going to find anything in the bathroom except baby aspirin for Bobby."

"Then I'll just haul you in for child abduction."

"You asshole," Ben said softly, so that Bobby wouldn't hear.

"If you say so," he said, flipping the book across the table to Ben. "By the way, Frank's not dead."

"What?" Ben gasped.

"I made some calls after we talked. The guy you found in the motel room? His name is Frank Baron and he's in the AIDS ward at County Hospital. You know what that means? If he was abusing Bobby the way you think he was, Bobby might be infected."

"You're lying."

"I wish I was," Gomez said. "Because even for L.A. this is some sick shit."

Ben muttered a shocked, "Oh, my God."

"This is way beyond you taking in a stray kid," Gomez said. "Bobby's the victim of a serious crime. You can't keep him here playing house with you. Get him ready to go, Ben. Let's not make this harder than it has to be."

ii.

"Mr. Manso? Good morning. I'm Elizabeth Lloyd."

The silken-haired woman who'd entered the tastefully decorated reception room where he'd been waiting for a half-hour wasn't at all what he'd expected from their brief conversations over the phone. To him, child psychologist conjured up the grandmotherly woman to whom he'd been sent at seven for his bed-wetting after he moved to Chicago with his mother. Elizabeth Lloyd wore a tailored wool suit of deep lavender and was as carefully coiffed and made-up as a model. It was easier for him to imagine her querying a wine steward than counseling troubled children.

"I'm sorry to keep you waiting," she said. She regarded him skeptically. "Bobby calls you the 'pretty man.' He's right."

Ben didn't take it as a compliment.

"I'd like to see him."

Since Gomez had removed an hysterical Bobby from Ben's apartment, Bobby had been at McMahon Hall, a holding facility for minors declared wards of the court.

"Come in," she said. "We'll talk."

He followed her into her office, which he had noted when she first gave him the address, was only a short walk from White Knights. The same muted colors and unobtrusive furnishings as were in the reception room prevailed here. He saw no signs to indicate her clients were children.

Ben slumped into an armchair upholstered in industrial gray.

"Talking to people is all I've been doing since the cops took Bobby," he complained. "Detectives, the D.A. I spent four hours at the D.A.'s office yesterday with three lawyers. Practice cross-examination, they called it. You wouldn't believe some of the things they asked me. They asked me if I abused Bobby."

"You're the D.A.'s star witness against Frank Baron," she said. "He has a very aggressive lawyer named Rios. The D.A. wants you to be ready for anything he might throw at you."

"Would he really ask me that? If I hurt Bobby?"

"You slept with him," she said.

Caught off-guard, Ben managed a startled, "What?"

"Bobby told me you slept in the same bed while he was staying with you."

"He was having nightmares," Ben said angrily.

"I'm sure it was completely innocent," she said, "but you can imagine how Baron's lawyer might twist that to suggest there was something improper going on between you and Bobby."

Ben grunted an incredulous, "That's sick."

"Henry Rios will do everything he can to tear you down in front of the jury," she said. "I should know. I've tangled with him before."

When he'd recovered his composure, he said, "I saw him on TV saying there was no evidence Baron abused Bobby."

Even though he was dying of AIDS at County Hospital, Frank Baron had been charged with multiple counts of lewd and lascivious conduct on a child under 14, which, if he was convicted, would insure that he died in prison. The case was national news. "Boy Allegedly Molested by AIDS Victim," the tamest headline had read, accompanied by a photograph showing the emaciated Baron handcuffed to his hospital bed. Rios, Baron's lawyer, had held a press conference where he claimed there was no medical evidence either that Bobby had been molested or that he was positive for the AIDS virus. Rios had left several messages on Ben's answering machine asking Ben to call him. The lead D.A. in charge of the prosecution had instructed him not to return Rios's calls. After what Lloyd had just told him about the lawyer, Ben was glad he hadn't.

"The medical evidence is inconclusive," Elizabeth Lloyd was saying. "It frequently is in these cases. Physically, children heal quickly."

"Is he infected?" Ben asked.

"The preliminary test was negative but since we don't know how recently Baron may have abused Bobby, that doesn't mean a subsequent test might not be positive." With a slight shrug, she added, "Anyway, whether he actually infected Bobby with HIV doesn't lessen his culpability for exposing the child to the virus. And physical evidence, aside, Bobby displays the classic behavioral symptoms of sexual abuse."

"Like what?"

She continued, sounding, he thought, as if she were practicing her testimony in court. "There's a pattern of behavior in children who've been abused we call the accommodation syndrome. The key element is secrecy and denial. Either the abuser has threatened the child to keep him quiet or the child keeps quiet out of feelings of shame and guilt. Baron took Bobby off the street and gave him a place to live. That's grooming behavior. It's meant to create trust between the child and the abuser, and to put the child in the abuser's debt. Once the abuse starts, and the trust is violated, the child feels helpless and will eventually accommodate himself to the situation because he sees no way out."

"But even after I got Bobby away from Frank, he wouldn't talk about what he did to him."

"That's not surprising, particularly for a male child. The shame is too great. He finds other ways to deal with it."

"Like what?"

"Bobby's created an alter ego."

Ben said, "I don't know what that means."

"Did he ever mention someone named Georgie to you?"

"Georgie? Yeah, he said that Georgie was his brother, but I figure he was either a pimp or another kid he met on the street."

"He was neither," she said with cool self-assurance. "Georgie is what Bobby calls the part of himself he can admit was abused."

"I don't understand. Did he tell you that?"

"Bobby told me the same thing he told you," she replied, "that he has a brother named Georgie who told him to stay with Baron. When I questioned him about Georgie, he said Georgie's step-father hurt him and he ran away and took Bobby with him."

"You think he made that up?"

"This story about Georgie," she said, "is what we call a confabulation, a kind of distorted version of reality that a trauma victim invents when the reality is too overwhelming to face. Bobby can't accept the fact he went willingly with his abuser, so he invented Georgie who told him to go with Baron, and then it was Georgie who was abused and who ran away from Baron and took Bobby with him." She shook her head. "It's text book, really. By inventing Georgie, Bobby has dissociated himself from the sexual abuse."

"Okay," Ben said, uncertainly. She spoke with such confidence that he assumed she knew what she was talking about, but some part of him remained unpersuaded. "But you said he talked about being beaten, not molested."

"Men," she said, "even little ones have a need to protect their masculinity. It's easier for them to admit they've been physically abused than sexually abused."

"But could there have been a Georgie?"

"He's been at McMahon for two weeks," she said, firmly. "No one has stepped forward to claim him, even with all the publicity surrounding the case. There is no Georgie. He's Georgie. I know instances of children who actually split into multiple personalities as a way of coping with their sexual abuse. This is just a milder form."

"I see," he said. "Can I visit him? The D.A. said she was okay with it, if you agreed."

She studied him. "You realize that if you do see him, he'll be angry at you for abandoning him."

"I didn't abandon him," Ben said angrily. "The cops took him away."

"That won't make any difference to him."

"If I can see him, he'll know I didn't abandon him. Please, doctor."

"All right," she said. "I'll arrange it."

On his way home from Lloyds's office, Ben stopped to see Iris Wong who had called him earlier in the week and said she needed to speak to him about Bobby. Her request surprised him since she had only been briefly involved, but she would not say over the phone what she wanted to talk to him about.

Her office was in Century City, in a glass tower, with a commanding view of the west side of the city all the way to ocean, which shimmered in the distance like a mirror. He gave his name to her receptionist, who recognized him from the times he had brought Wade in for an appointment. They chatted briefly about the unexpectedly cool late August weather and then he sat down and picked up a two month old *People* magazine.

"Ben?" Iris stood at the door to the waiting room, her white smock covering a black pants suit.

"Hi," he said, closing the magazine.

"Come into my office."

He followed her past her examining rooms into a small office. He took the chair in front of her cluttered desk. On the wall behind her, beside her framed university and medical school degrees—both from UCLA—was an antique Chinese scroll depicting two tiny human figures ascending a mountainous landscape. He had sat in her office many times with Wade looking at the scroll; the tiny figures never seemed to make any headway.

"How is Wade?" she asked, briskly.

"He's fine," he said, then added, "Well, you know, he's fine for Wade. Still can't get him off his Milano cookie diet."

She nodded. "As long as he's taking his medications?"

"I make sure of that. You wanted to talk to me about Bobby."

"Yes," she said, drawing a breath. "I did. Have you seen him?"

"Not yet. I just finished talking to his shrink."

"Elizabeth Lloyd?" she asked, with distaste.

"Yeah," he said, surprised. "You talk to her, too?"

"She called me since I was the first doctor to examine Bobby. She insisted on telling me what I saw."

"What do you mean?"

"She wanted me to tell her about physical signs of sexual abuse. I told her," she said coldly, as if still talking to Lloyd, "I didn't see any. All I saw was a hungry, sick, frightened kid."

"Did you look at Bobby to see if he had, you know, been molested?" he asked awkwardly.

"Not at first, but then after you told me you thought he'd been abused, I went back into the bedroom and took another look at him."

Ben nodded, remembering how, after he had told her his story at his apartment, she had excused herself and returned to the bedroom.

"I specifically looked for signs of sexual abuse. Of course, under the circumstances, I couldn't do a thorough examination because I didn't want to traumatize him further. But I didn't see anything obvious"

"What were you looking for?"

"Scarring or enlargement of his anus, tenderness around his abdomen, any sign of venereal disease."

"Lloyd told me that kids heal fast."

Iris raised a dismissive eyebrow. "You don't heal without scars."

"She said the scars were inside. She said he behaved like a kid who'd been abused."

"You mean her spiel about child sexual accommodation syndrome."

"You don't believe her?"

Iris sank back into her chair with a thoughtful look. "It isn't that I don't believe abused kids may have some common behaviors, but psychology isn't a hard science. A behavior, even a cluster of behaviors, can indicate any number of things are going on in a patient and not necessarily the label a psychologist gives it. This accommodation syndrome was only identified a few years ago. There aren't a lot of studies about its validity."

"Why would a kid lie about being abused?"

"He might not lie," she said, "but kids are impressionable and they want to please adults so they can be pretty easily coached. Look at what happen in the McMartin case. Those kids claimed they were forced to participate in Satanic rituals but it turns out they were simply repeating what the prosecutor wanted them to say. Besides," she continued, "as I understand it, Bobby has never said to anyone he was molested by Baron."

"Lloyd said that's part of the behavior."

"See, that's what I mean about this so-called syndrome," she said, leaning forward and tapping an impatient finger on her desk. "According to her, if he says he was abused, he was abused and if he doesn't say he was abused, he was abused. This isn't a syndrome, it's a catch-twenty two."

He flushed angrily. "That's for you two to fight over. All I know is something bad happened to Bobby when he was out on the streets."

"I don't doubt that," she said, quietly. "But Ben, a quarter of my patients are HIV positive. This story about a sexual predator infecting a little boy has generated all kinds of anti-AIDS hysteria. Some of these men are terrified if they disclose their status, they'll be called child molesters. Do you really want to be part of that?"

"Baron did something to him," he insisted. "He should be punished for it."

"But where is the evidence that he did what you, and everyone else, thinks he did?" she replied with equal firmness. "Anyway, what I wanted to tell you is that the prosecution isn't going to call me at Baron's trial after what I told Lloyd. I'll be testifying for the defense."

"How can you do that?" he demanded. "Baron's lawyer is a complete slime ball."

"Have you spoken to him?"

"No," Ben replied, "but Lloyd and the D.A. think he's going to be say I molested Bobby."

"I spoke to him," she said. "He seems like a decent guy. I can't imagine he would suggest anything like that. Anyway, Ben, I saw no evidence Bobby was sexually abused. The jury needs to hear that."

"You're unbelievable," he said, and stormed out of her office.

He and Bobby were walking across the grounds of McMahon Hall toward the high wire fence that surrounded the place. Behind them, obscured by mist, was a lumpy brown-brick edifice with turrets and guard towers. He heard dogs barking and he and the boy began to run. Heart beating frantically, he saw a fence ahead of them and put out his hand, grasping it. An electric shock knocked him to his knees. He pulled himself free and shouted to Bobby, "Don't touch it!"

Glancing over his shoulder, Ben could make out the dark forms of the dogs galloping through the mist.

"Fly!" he yelled at the terrified boy, and flapped his own arms to show him how. "Fly!"

The boy flapped his thin arms wildly, like a cartoon character. They began to rise from the ground, slowly at first, but with increasing speed.

"Fly!" Ben shouted, ecstatic now as they easily surmounted the fence, rising above the mist into the clear blue sky. He looked over at Bobby who laughed wildly as he darted through the air, his arms beating as fast as a hummingbird's wings.

"Fly," Ben said. "Fly, fly..."

He woke to the darkness.

"I brought these for you," Ben said producing from his pocket He-Man and Skeletor.

Unsmilingly, Bobby took the figures, murmuring, "I left them for when I come home."

Ben said, "I thought you might want them to keep you company here but I can take them back if you want."

Bobby shook his head.

"Anyway, I brought you a present, too."

Bobby reluctantly accepted the brightly colored package. He had not met Ben's eyes since Ben had arrived for their visit.

"Aren't you going to open it?"

Without replying, the boy unwrapped the present, opened the box, and examined the Masters of the Universe sweatshirt that Ben had brought him.

He mumbled, "Thank you."

Ben felt Bobby withdrawing from him and he was helpless to stop it. Unlike the place in his dream, McMahon Hall didn't have turrets and guard towers. It looked like an elementary school, boxy rectangular buildings connected by covered hallways. They were in the cafeteria, a high-ceilinged building that smelled of stewed tomatoes and disinfectant. From its banks of windows was a view of the grounds. And a fence. It was not as ominous as it had been in Ben's dream, but it was there.

"Bobby, I'm sorry they made you come here. I tried to stop them."

The boy looked stubbornly away.

"I came to see you as soon as I could."

"I hate it here," Bobby said. "They call me AIDS boy. They make me eat by myself over there." He pointed to a small table in the corner with a single chair. "The other kids throw food at me and say stuff like, *When are you gonna die, AIDS boy?*" He met Ben's eyes for the first time. "Am I going to die, Ben?"

"No," he said. "You don't have AIDS and you're not going to die."

In a miserable whisper he said, "Sometimes I want to."

"You can't think that way, Bobby," Ben said. "You won't be here forever. I promise you. Come on, let's go for a walk." He extended the sweatshirt to the boy. "Put this on *m'ijo*, it's cold outside."

Bobby took the sweatshirt and pulled it over his head, making his hair stick up in every direction. Ben used his fingers to comb it while Bobby watched him with hurt eyes. They walked across the grounds toward the fence, not speaking. When they reached the fence, Ben put out his hand and brushed his fingertips against it, half-expecting a shock, but felt only cold metal.

"I know you want out of here," he said.

Bobby grabbed the fence and pulled himself back and forth against it. "I want to go home with you."

"That's what I want, too," Ben said, "but these people think your family might come to take you home. Don't you miss your family?"

"I miss you," Bobby said.

Ben sat down, his back against the fence. Bobby stood next to him, looking at him gravely. Ben reached up his hand and pulled Bobby down, hugging the boy to him. "I miss you, too," he said, his voice breaking. "I miss you so much."

Bobby buried his face in Ben's chest and they wept.

"Please, Ben," Bobby said, his face muffled against Ben's chest. "Please take me with you."

Ben dried his face on his sleeve and said, "You have to tell them what Frank did to you."

"He didn't do nothing," Bobby protested.

"Bobby," Ben said, "he can't hurt you anymore."

Bobby extricated himself from their embrace and sat between Ben's legs, his back against Ben's chest, Ben's arms encircling him. "That lady wants me to say that Frank put his thing in me," he said.

"Miss Lloyd?"

"Uh-huh," Bobby said.

"If that's what he did," Ben said, "then that's what you have to tell her. Don't be embarrassed. Just tell the truth."

Bobby leaned back against Ben's chest and after a thoughtful silence, asked, "Then I could go home with you?"

Ben pulled him closer. "I promise you we'll be a family again."

When he got home, Ben found Wade pacing the hall in his walker. Today he wore a maroon running suit of plush velour and a pink bandanna tied ascot-style around his neck.

"Just in time for tea," Wade said, reaching out with talon like fingers to grip Ben's hand.

"Sure," Ben said. He helped the old man into his rocker and went into the kitchen to put the kettle on.

"How was your visit?" Wade asked when he returned to the living room.

Ben lit a cigarette and sat down. "I should have run with him when I had the chance."

"That's kidnapping, baby. No matter how good your intentions are, it's still against the law."

"The law," Ben said contemptuously. "The law doesn't care about Bobby."

"It wants to punish the man who hurt him," Wade said.

"The guy's dying of AIDS," Ben replied. "Have you seen what that's like? Maybe that's punishment enough. And what will happen to Bobby after the law finishes with him? He'll either stay in juvie or end up in foster care unless I can get him back somehow."

"It doesn't look like he has anyone else, Ben.

"I know," he said, "but I'm not exactly foster dad material. It didn't take Gomez long to figure out I was a whore."

"Ex-whore," Wade observed.

Ben grinned mirthlessly. "Yeah, ex-whore. How much difference will that make to the law if I try to get custody?"

The tea-kettle whistled. He went back into the kitchen, prepared a pot of Twining's Earl Grey, bringing it out on a tray with two cups, sugar, milk, and a plate of Milano cookies.

"Even if you can't get custody," Wade said, blowing over the surface of his tea, "you saved his life. He would have died on the streets if you hadn't taken him in."

"It would kill me if I lost him for good," Ben said. "I think about him all the time."

"That's what happens when you love someone," Wade replied.

"Yeah," Ben said, adding, "you were right about my dad, Wade."

"Beg pardon?"

"When I told you he died, you said he didn't do it to hurt me. I understand that now. He didn't want to leave me, but he couldn't help it. I can, with Bobby," he said. "I don't know how, but I'm going to come through for him."

A few days later, Ben called Elizabeth Lloyd to check on Bobby.

"I'm so glad you called me," she said, her cool tone belying her enthusiasm. "I've got some great news about Bobby."

"What's that?"

"Well, first, he was finally able to talk about the abuse."

"Really? When did that happen?"

"At one of our sessions earlier this week," she replied.

"What did he tell you?"

"Well, it was all rather general," she said, reverting to her tone of cool assessment, "but

at one point he did say—I'm using his words—
that Frank put his dick in Bobby's butt. He's
unclear as to dates and times, but children
often are."

Ben wondered if he should mention he had
told Bobby he had to tell her about the abuse,
but quickly dismissed the thought—he hadn't
coached the boy, he had only told him was to
tell the truth.

"There's more news, too," Lloyd was
saying. "Bobby's mother has come forward."

It took a moment for Ben to understand.
"His what?"

"His mother. She identified his picture in
the newspaper."

"His picture's been in the paper for weeks,"
Ben said.

"Not in Santa Barbara county," she replied.
"That's where Bobby's from, a small town
called Guadalupe. Apparently, some neighbor
saw Bobby's picture in the *Times* and brought
it to her. She's coming down today."

"To take him home?"

"Presumably," Lloyd said.

"Are you sure she's his mother?"

"Well, I can't be sure until I talk to her,"
she replied, a bit tartly. "You know, Ben, your

attitude toward all this is really quite curious. I thought you'd be happy."

"I am."

"You don't sound it," she said. "I have to go now—"

"Wait, will I be able to see him?"

"Once he's back with his family, that's out of my hands," she said. "I'll tell his mother you asked. It'll be up to her."

"Tonight, we have a happy ending to a sad story."

Ben turned up the volume on the TV and leaned back into the pillow, glass of bourbon in hand, watching the white-haired anchor on the local news arrange his face into happy crinkles.

"Tonight, little Bobby Velez was reunited with his family. Bobby, you will remember, is the child who was allegedly sexually abused by a man suffering from AIDS. We go to Tom Jasper for the story."

The scene switched to McMahon Hall. A coiffed male mannequin—whom Ben had seen in the backroom of a leather bar in Silver Lake orally servicing all takers—looked sincerely into the camera.

"Four weeks ago, eight-year-old Bobby was brought to McMahon Hall after police discovered that he'd been living with a man, Frank Baron, who has AIDS."

"Bullshit," Ben slurred at the screen. "I found him."

"Subsequent investigation revealed that Bobby had been sexually abused by the man who is now in critical condition from the disease in the jail ward of County Hospital. Even though Baron is dying, the D.A. decided to press child molestation charges against him."

There was a quick shot of the press conference at which the D.A. had announced charges. "Heinous," he was saying. "Unbelievable."

"Since then, Bobby has been here, at McMahon Hall, while investigators hoped that publicity surrounding the case would turn up Bobby's parents. Today their hopes were realized when Bobby's mother, Maria Torres, stepped forward to claim her son."

There was a shot of a heavy woman in a dark dress, tears running down her face, embracing Bobby, who looked dazed.

"Tonight, Bobby, now reunited with his family, is en route home just in time for the beginning of the school year. This is Tom Jasper at McMahon Hall."

"Tom," the anchor asked, "how will Bobby's reunion with his family affect the case against Frank Baron?"

Jasper said, "It won't. The D.A.'s office intends to go forward with the case and at some point Bobby will have to return to Los Angeles to testify at the trial."

"Thank you, Tom," the anchor said.

"*Thank you, Tom*," Ben mimicked, drunkenly.

After a week of silence, Ben called Elizabeth Lloyd. It took him several tries to get through to her. When he did, she was even brisker than usual.

"I wanted to know if I can see Bobby," Ben explained. "You were going to talk to his mother."

"I did," Lloyd said. "Obviously if she hasn't contacted you it's because she doesn't want you to see him."

"Could you give me her phone number, so I can talk to her?"

There was a pause. "I'm sorry, Ben, I really can't do that."

"What the hell's going on here? I'm the star witness, remember?"

"Detective Gomez told Mrs. Torres he found Bobby with you and she wanted to know more about you," she said. "Evidently, based on their conversation she's decided it wouldn't be in Bobby's best interests for him to have any further contact with you."

"What did Gomez tell her?" Ben demanded.

"I think you know what he told her," she replied coolly.

"That's all behind me now," he said. When she didn't respond, he added, "I got Bobby off the streets. I took care of him. Doesn't that count for something?"

"Not legally," she replied.

"Screw legally."

"I really have to go, Ben."

"I'll remember this when you people need me to testify at the trial."

"I don't think you'll have to worry about that," she replied.

"What's that supposed to mean?"

"You'll have to excuse me," she said curtly and hung up.

"Fuck you," he replied to the dial tone.

That night he made dinner for Wade. He was angrily tearing apart pieces of lettuce for salad when Wade called, "Ben, get out here. Hurry!"

Wiping his hands on his jeans, he went to the doorway. "What?"

"The news," Wade said, pointing at the screen.

"With Baron's death, the case against him will now be closed," the reporter, standing outside the criminal court building, was saying. "That's according to his lawyer, Henry Rios."

The scene shifted to a tall, thin, dark-skinned man in a rumpled suit standing in a hospital corridor. He said, "I've filed a motion to dismiss all charges. The D.A.'s office has indicated it won't contest it. I'm sorry to see the case end this way because I was prepared to prove that there was no truth to these allegations."

A reporter shouted, "What do you mean? Didn't the boy tell authorities your client sexually abused him."

"That statement was the result of coaching by the prosecutor's expert," Rios replied. "That would have come out during the trial, along with the fact there was no evidence of sexual abuse and that the boy has consistently tested negative for the HIV virus. There is a tragic story here," the lawyer continued, "but it wasn't the one the prosecutor was telling. All the D.A.'s office accomplished with these bogus charges was to enflame prejudice against people suffering with AIDS."

"What's the real story then?" the reporter asked skeptically.

The lawyer paused before saying, "That's a private matter now, for the child's family. I only hope his family does right by him."

Back in the studio the anchor said, "To repeat, Frank Baron, the AIDS victim accused of sexually molesting an eight-year-old boy, died today in the jail ward of County Hospital."

Ben stared at the screen. "That's what Lloyd meant about the trial. She knew Baron was about to die. I've got to talk to that lawyer."

"What about?" Wade asked.

"The real story."

Henry Rios's office was on a run-down section of Sunset, just west of Vine in a square, pinkish three-story building, flanked on one side by a coffee shop and on the other by a store-front psychic. In the little foyer, a tiled wall mosaic depicted a school of fish swimming in the direction of the elevator. Ben pushed the elevator button and waited. After five minutes he climbed the stairs to the top floor where a simple metal plaque affixed to the door to room 311 announced *Henry Rios, Attorney-at-Law.* In the small reception area, a handsome black woman in a brightly colored silk dress and cornrows was working at a computer.

She glanced up at Ben, her fingers paused over the keyboard and asked, "Hello, may I help you?"

"Yeah, I'm Ben Manso. I have an appointment to see Henry Rios."

She picked up the phone and pressed three digits. "Ben Manso is here." To Ben she said, "The end of the hall."

"Thanks," he said, and stepped around her desk. At the end of a short, linoleum covered hall was the door to Rios's office. The door was open but Ben knocked anyway.

Rios said, "Come in, Ben."

In the office, the linoleum gave way to tweedy gray carpeting. Along the street side was a bank of grime-streaked windows, half of them opened, that let in cool air and mid-

morning light. Beneath the windows was
a black leather couch and a coffee table; a
couple of throw pillows covered in Turkish
carpet fabric were stacked at one end of the
couch. The couch held the faint impression of
a prone body. The possibility that the lawyer
sometimes napped there relieved some of the
anxiety Ben felt about coming to see him.

Rios sat behind an elegant kidney-shaped
table. The top was wood stained black and it
was supported by red metal legs; a computer
console in the same style supported a desktop
computer. His chair was upholstered in red
leather and he had hung his suit jacket over
the back. Behind him was a stainless steel
console table covered with books and files
and a framed photograph of Rios with his arm
around a younger man. They looked nothing
like each other and yet they seemed related.

Rios stood up from behind his desk. He
was Ben's height, six feet or so, and slender.
His clothes were a bit wrinkled and a bit loose
but Ben detected a strong, wiry body when he
leaned forward to shake Ben's hand. He was
darker-skinned than he appeared on television
and his face both sharper and more delicately
boned. His black hair was streaked with gray

but Ben thought he was probably, at most, in his late thirties. He was austerely handsome and he would have been intimidating were it not for his eyes, which were bright and inquisitive and kind.

"Hello, Ben," he said, shaking Ben's hand across the desk. "Have a seat. I'm glad you called."

Ben slipped into one of the comfortably padded chairs facing the desk and said, defensively, "The D.A.'s office told me not to talk to you before."

"Yes, I know. They were afraid you might say something to me I could use against you at trial. Is that what they told you?"

"The D.A said you'd accuse me of molesting Bobby."

An angry expression flashed across his face. "That's contemptible. I fight hard for my clients, but I fight within the rules. That doesn't include accusing witnesses of crimes I know they didn't commit."

"Dr. Lloyd said you would have made me out to be a liar."

He shook his head. "They really worked you over didn't they. If we had gone to trial, and I had cross-examined you, I would have got you to admit that Bobby never told you Frank Baron molested him, and that your belief he had been molested, which is what you told Gomez, was nothing more than your assumption. Isn't that what happened?"

"Yeah," Ben conceded, "but then he told Dr. Lloyd that Baron molested him."

"That's true," Rios replied. "He did say that, finally, after consistently telling her that Frank hadn't done anything to him." He opened a file. "This is the log of Bobby's visitors at McMahon. You visited him just before he changed his story." He gazed levelly at Ben. "What did you tell him?"

"To tell the truth," Ben said, uncomfortably.

"To tell the truth about what?" Rios persisted in a quiet voice.

"About what Baron did to him."

Rios had not changed his mild expression but his dark eyes were focused and probing as he asked, "And did you tell Bobby that if he changed his story he could come home with you."

"How did you know that?" Ben exclaimed.

Rios leaned back in his chair, breaking the tension that had arisen between them. He smiled. "I didn't until now, but I figured it was something like that. Iris Wong told me you lied to her about reporting Bobby to the authorities because you wanted to give him a home with you. I also got summaries of Lloyd's notes of her interviews with him and he asked her, more than once, when he could be reunited with you. Obviously, you and Bobby have a deep bond. The fact that he changed his story after you visited him suggested an inducement and the strongest one I could think of was a promise that, if he told Dr. Lloyd what she wanted to hear, Bobby could come home with you."

"I didn't tell him to lie," Ben protested.

"I know you didn't, Ben, because you honestly believed that Frank had molested Bobby. Unfortunately, you're wrong."

"How can you be so sure?" Ben demanded. "Did Baron tell you that?"

With a slight shake of his head and a sigh, Rios said, "Frank had AIDS-related dementia. He wasn't able to tell me much of anything. That's why it took me so long to figure out what actually happened."

"What did happen?" Ben asked. "How did he end up with Bobby?"

Rios said, "He's Bobby's father."

Ben managed a stunned, "What!"

"Did Bobby ever talk to you about his brother, Georgie?"

Startled, Ben said, "Yeah, but Dr. Lloyd said there wasn't any Georgie. She said Bobby made him up."

Rios managed a smile that was both polite and dismissive. "Dr. Lloyd is what you might call a professional witness in child abuse cases. As a witness she can be very persuasive but as a psychologist, she's wrong as often as she is right." He leaned back into his chair. The noise of traffic drifted up from the street. "She's certainly wrong about Georgie. At this moment, Georgie Velez is doing a two year sentence at the California Men's Colony for burglary."

"Bobby's brother?"

Rios nodded. "Yes. What did Bobby tell you about Georgie?"

Ben thought back. "He said he came with Georgie to L.A. after their stepdad beat Georgie up. Is that true, too?"

"Yes," Rios said. "Georgie and Bobby were the children of their mother's first marriage, to Emilio Velez. When they got divorced, she remarried this man, Tiburcio Torres, who, as far as I can gather, hated the boys. He and Georgie had a violent relationship. Two years ago, when Georgie was sixteen, Torres beat him so badly, he ended up in the hospital. When Georgie got out he decided that he'd had enough and he ran away. He took Bobby with him because he was afraid if he left him there, Torres would start on him."

"Why did they come to L.A.?"

"Because Georgie found out that their father was here. They came here to find him."

"Why did their parents split up?" Ben asked. "Why didn't their dad take the boys with him?"

Rios said, "Now that's a long story."

"Please, Mr. Rios, I want to understand."

"Henry," Rios said. "Call me Henry." He paused for a moment as if gathering his thoughts, then said. "Okay, let me tell this in the proper order. Emilio got Maria pregnant with Georgie when they were still in high school and their families insisted that they drop out and get married. Which they did. The problem was that, while they were married, Emilio figured out he was gay. Now," Rios continued, "it's one thing to figure that out if you're on your own and living in a big city, but quite another to discover it when you're a Mexican-American high school dropout, married with a kid, working in a cannery, and living in a blue collar town where your family and everyone you've ever known lives. Your options are limited."

"What did he do?"

"He came here," Rios said. "To L.A. He told Maria it was to find better work but it was really so he could come out of the closet. But his job prospects weren't much better here than in Guadalupe and he was a small town guy in a big, lonely city, so he went back. For awhile, and then he left again. He did that for several years, going back and forth between Guadalupe and L.A. and somewhere along the line he got hooked on heroin. The last time he was in Guadalupe, two things happened. He got Maria pregnant again—with Bobby—and one of his brothers discovered him having sex with another man. After that, Emilio left Guadalupe for good. By this time he was a junkie and an outcast and obviously in no position to take care of his sons. Maria remarried, this man, Torres. He despised her sons because they were the children of a *maricón*."

"A what?" Ben asked.

"A queer," Rios said, biting off the word. "You see, in Guadalupe, the sins of the father are visited on the sons. The boys had to live with the stigma of their father's disgrace not only in the community, but in their own home. Torres would bad-mouth Emilio and Georgie would defend him. Eventually, their arguments escalated into violence. So Georgie left, taking Bobby with him."

"To find their dad, you said. How?"

"While they were still married, Emilio would write Maria, sending money or asking for it. Georgie got his father's address off one of the old letters."

"Did they find him?"

"No, the address was to the county jail."

"Their dad was a criminal?"

"Their dad was a junkie who fed his habit with petty crime. Theft, hustling. He was in and out of jail." He straightened a pile of papers on his desk. "I met him when I was appointed to represent him after he was busted for prostitution. I worked out a plea, got him into rehab, encouraged him to get clean. He'd go straight for awhile but the guilt and shame of being gay and what he'd done to his family always drove him back to drugs. I could never convince him there was no shame in being gay. That shame, it was the real poison, not the heroin."

Ben glanced at the photo of Rios and the younger man and thought with sudden clarity, *His lover. He's gay.*

Rios continued, "Georgie didn't know what to do when he realized his dad was in jail, but he was understandably afraid to go home, so the boys stayed in L.A. Eventually, they drifted to Hollywood, like a lot of runaways. Georgie supported them the way street kids do, the same way his father kept himself alive. They did this for about a year. Then, one of Georgie's friends got picked up and sent to county. Georgie asked him to look for his father. He found him."

Ben interrupted. "What about Bobby? Did he do that stuff? Hustling?"

"Georgie says no, and I believe him," Rios replied. "I think he tried to shield him from the worst part of living on the street but I imagine Bobby still saw a lot of things no child should have to see. He's not a tough kid."

Ben nodded. "No, he isn't."

"When their dad got out of county, he and the boys reunited. But, Emilio saw the kind of life they were living and told Georgie to take Bobby and go home to Guadalupe. Georgie refused and they ended up hiding from Emilio, too. Then Georgie was arrested for trying to break into a Taco Bell or some such thing. When they sent him up to jail, he got word to his dad and made him promise to take care of Bobby until he got out." Rios paused and looked at Ben. "Emilio Velez had a lot of aliases. The one he was going by after he got out of jail this last time was Frank Baron."

"Frank was Emilio?"

"That's right," Rios said. "And he was Bobby's dad. Unfortunately, when he took Bobby in Frank had AIDS though he didn't know it at the time. He had lived a high risk life without any access to medical care so when the infections starting coming, they hit him hard and fast. He got very ill very quickly and Bobby was pretty much on his own. And that's where you came in, and misunderstood the situation. You took Bobby away from his father and told the cops Frank had abused him."

"I thought Frank was dead."

"He wasn't," Rios said, "but he was hardly in any shape to tell the cops the true story, so all they had was what you told them and based on that they charged him with these terrible crimes."

"But you knew the truth," Ben said. "Why didn't you tell the cops?"

Rios shook his head. "I didn't know the whole story until just recently. I knew Frank came from Guadalupe, but not the details. I had to piece the story together from Bobby's statements to the police and from the little bit I could get out of Frank when he was coherent. It was just a couple of days before Frank died that I found Georgie at the men's colony and drove up to see him. By the time I had the complete picture, Frank was dead and then, of course, it was too late for it to help him. Had you talked to me earlier, when I first called you, and told me about Georgie then, I might have figured it out sooner."

"I'm sorry," Ben said.

Rios leaned back in his chair, fatigue informing the lines around his eyes. "Even if I had known the whole story before Frank died, I'm not sure it would have prevented the D.A. from prosecuting him. They had you and Lloyd telling them Frank molested Bobby and AIDS hysteria to contend with so the D.A. might have figured it was a better move politically to go to trial and force me to put on my defense rather than dismiss the charges even if they knew Frank was innocent."

"But you would have got him off," Ben said.

"My client was a homosexual junkie with AIDS," Rios said. "For some jurors that would have been enough to convict him of any crime the prosecutor charged him with."

"That's messed up," Ben said.

"These are the times we live in," Rios replied. "And the law is never any better than the people who enforce it."

"What about Bobby?" Ben asked. "The law gave him back to his mom. Do you think he's safe there?"

"No," Rios said. "That's why I called Child Services in Santa Barbara and had a long conversation with a social worker about Bobby's situation."

"What did they say?"

Rios massaged his temple. "She said she'd do a welfare check on him."

"When?" Ben demanded.

"I don't know," Rios admitted. "Look, Ben, the law goes to extraordinary lengths to keep parents and their children together."

"Maybe it shouldn't," Ben said, bitterly. "Not if the parents are the ones the kid should be afraid of."

"I don't disagree with you," Rios replied. "I can think of a lot of kids who might be better off if the law was more protective of their rights to safety than their parents' right to custody."

"Like gay kids?" Ben asked, meeting Rios's eyes.

"Yes," Rios said. "Like them."

"Like you said, Bobby's not tough. He won't run away. If his mom won't protect him from his stepfather, no one will."

"There's an interesting thing about his mom," Rios said, thoughtfully, "Mrs. Torres didn't report her boys missing when Georgie and Bobby ran away. Had her neighbor not forced the issue by showing her Bobby's picture in the paper, I don't think she would have made any effort to find him."

"Because she knew that wherever he was, he was better off than with her husband and her?" Ben asked.

"That's certainly one explanation," Rios said. "Look, if the stepfather beat the kids, he probably beat their mother, too. Someone like Mrs. Torres—poor, no education, no prospects—may not think she has option but to stay with the guy. Maybe the only way she could protect her boys was to let them go."

Ben thought about it and asked, "If she did it once, would she do it again?"

"What, let Bobby run away? You just said he won't do that."

"But what if," Ben said, "someone rescued him."

Rios looked at him gravely. "Even if he went willingly, it would still be child abduction."

"Have you looked at a milk carton lately? Kids disappear all the time."

"It's still a crime."

"What's the punishment for child abduction?" Ben asked.

"That would depend," Rios replied. "on whether the D.A. decided to prosecute it as a misdemeanor or a felony. A misdemeanor is punishable by up to a year, a felony by up to four years."

"Four years? That's not so long."

"Listen, Ben," he said warily. "You need to be very careful about what you say to me here. I'm an officer of the court. I can't be compelled to disclose anything a client accused of a crime tells me, even if he confesses. But I can't shield someone who tells me he's planning to commit a crime. Of course," Rios continued, "if you're just talking hypothetically, that's another matter. I mean, hypothetically, I could see why someone who loved a kid, but had no legal right to custody, would want to rescue him from a violent father."

Ben nodded. "Yeah, I was only talking, you know, hypothetically."

"He'd have to be someone who could vanish himself without leaving any traces."

"Like a street person," Ben said. "Someone you see but don't notice."

"Yeah," Rios said. "Someone like that. He'd have to take the kid somewhere where they weren't known or likely to raise suspicion. Probably not a small town."

"No," Ben said. "A city, a different city, I mean, than the one they came from."

Rios, opened a file, shuffled through some papers, and then wrote something on a yellow legal pad. "I have no idea when this social worker will get around to checking up on Bobby, but if you want to visit him to see that he's okay, this is where he's living."

He slid the paper across the desk to Ben. Ben read the address, folded the paper and slipped it into his pocket. "Thanks, maybe I'll do that."

"If you do see Bobby, Georgie will want to know how he's doing. You can reach him through me."

Ben got up to go. "Thank you," he said.

"Good luck, Ben," Rios said. "I hope you never need my services, but if you do, for any reason, you know where to find me."

Iris stepped into her reception room where Ben had been waiting for a break between her appointments see her. "Hello, Ben," she said. "Is something wrong with Wade?"

"No," he said. "Can I talk to you privately."

She led him back to her office. He sat down and glanced at the scroll on the wall behind her where the old sages had made no progress up the side of the mountain.

"It's about Bobby," he said.

She frowned. "What about him? Isn't he's back with his family?"

"He's in the hospital."

"What happened?" she asked, alarmed.

"I don't know," Ben said. "That's why I came to see you."

Puzzled, she said, "I don't understand , Ben."

"Yeah, I guess I should start from the beginning," he replied and told her about his visit with Rios earlier in the week and how, the day after, he had driven to Guadalupe. "I found the house. Bobby's mom answered the door. Lloyd told me the D.A. had said some things to her about me and that's why she wouldn't let me see Bobby before she took him back to Guadalupe, but Lloyd lied to me. Mrs. Torres had no idea who I was."

She had been pretty once but now her face sagged, her hair was flecked with gray and her eyes were dull and tired. A little girl, no more than three, clung to the hem of her dress and a baby wailed from a room within the small house on a street without sidewalks or street lights in a town of pawn shops, bars, and businesses advertising in Spanish.

"*I found Bobby on the streets after Frank got sick,*" Ben told her when she said she had never heard of him. "*He was digging in the* garbage for food. I took care of him until the cops came and took him away from me."

"You gave him those dolls," she said, accusingly.

"What dolls?" Ben asked, confused.

"Those little men he was playing with when my husband—" she stopped herself. "Why did you have to give him dolls?"

She seemed not so much angry as frightened.

"They're just toys," Ben said, confused.

"I asked her if I could see Bobby," Ben told Iris. "That's when she told me Bobby was hurt."

"What happened to him?" Ben asked.

Fear brightened the dull eyes. "He fell and broke his arm," she said. "He's in the hospital."

He knew immediately she was lying about how Bobby had hurt himself. He resisted the urge to shake the truth out of her and said, "I'm sorry to hear that. I'd still like to see him. Which hospital is he in?"

She shook her head. "No, I don't think that's a good idea."

"Why not?"

"I just, I don't think, you know, my husband wouldn't like it."

"Well, maybe I could stick around and ask your husband when he gets home," Ben said.

Fear lit her eyes again. "My husband don't like me talking to strangers. You should go now."

"I'm not a stranger," Ben said. "I'm Bobby's friend. I want to make sure he's okay."

A thin, aproned woman came out of the next door house and stood on her porch, arms at her hips, watching them. The fear in Mrs. Torres's eyes became panic.

"That's my sister-in-law," she breathed anxiously. "You gotta go now."

"Tell me the name of the hospital and I'll leave," Ben said.

She shook her head, stepped back into the house and slammed the door shut. He could feel the sister-in-law's glare and, without looking at her, went to his car and drove away.

"There aren't hospitals in Guadalupe," he said. "The nearest ones are in Santa Barbara. That's why I came to see you."

"I don't understand," Iris said.

"You were Bobby's doctor," he said. "Is there some way you could find out where they took him?"

She frowned. "I wasn't really Bobby's doctor."

"If you said you were, and called the hospitals in Santa Barbara, they would tell you if he was there, wouldn't they? I tried, but they wouldn't give me any information."

"What do you think happened to him?" she asked.

"Isn't it obvious?" he said. "His stepfather hurt him because he was playing with dolls. We need to find him and get him out that house before he's killed."

"How are you going to do that?"

"Mr. Rios said he told Child Services in Santa Barbara about Bobby's stepfather. If he put Bobby in the hospital, they'd have to do something."

She looked at him steadily. "You could report the stepfather now," she said, "and Child Services would investigate."

"His mom isn't going to say anything and Bobby won't talk to a stranger, but he'll talk to me."

After a moment, she said, "I'll see what I can do."

He and Wade were in Wade's apartment watching "Gilda" when Iris called.

"He's at St. Martin's hospital in Santa Barbara," she said, "They brought him in with a broken arm, fractured ribs and a mild concussion. His mother said he fell. He's due to be released in a couple of days."

"Thank you," Ben said.

She hung up.

Wade looked over at him from the bundle of blankets and afghans with which he'd covered himself. "Who was that?"

"Wrong number."

Wade raised a disbelieving eyebrow.

"I'm going away tomorrow, Wade," Ben said. "I won't be back."

"Bobby?" the old man asked.

"The police will be coming around. The less you know the better."

"You'd be surprised at how well I perform the senile old man bit." He smiled sadly. "I'll miss you, baby."

"I'll miss you, too, Wade."

"Are you sure you're ready to be a father?" Wade asked him.

Ben said, "No, but I'm ready to try."

Ben lay awake that night devising elaborate plans of how to get Bobby out of the hospital, but in the end, simplicity won out. The next morning, he packed a bag and went up to Santa

Barbara where he spent the day at the hospital, observing the shift changes and mealtimes, watching for the moment of maximum confusion. It happened just after lunch. The halls were crowded with orderlies pushing carts of dirty dishes, doctors making their rounds, and visitors coming in for afternoon visiting hours. Everyone moved with a specific purpose, blind to the traffic around them.

He bought a pair of scrubs at a uniform store and went back the following day with a sack of clothes for the boy. He pushed a wheelchair into Bobby's room and told him they were leaving. Bobby nodded, as if he'd known Ben would come all along. He helped Bobby get dressed and into the wheelchair. Ben pushed him through the crowded halls toward the entrance. They were scarcely noticed in the din and bustle, a little boy with a broken arm and an orderly taking him somewhere, to do something. No one noticed them leave nor get into the car nor saw the car drive off. It wasn't until much later that afternoon, when Mrs. Torres came to visit, that the disappearance was discovered. To the hospital administration's embarrassment, no one could say what had happened.

Much later, Bobby told Ben that his stepfather had found him playing with He-Man and Skeletor and become enraged telling him only girls and sissies played with dolls. He demanded them but Bobby refused to give them up because they were all he had left to remind him of Ben. That's when his stepfather had attacked him.

Mrs. Torres never told the police about the man who had come asking about her son. Bobby's abduction from the hospital made the news in L.A., briefly. Ed Gomez saw the story and remembered Ben Manso but when he finally got around to following up, Ben had moved and left no forwarding address. He questioned Ben's neighbors who told him Ben had been friends with the old man who lived downstairs, but the fluttery old queen was no help. Without any evidence to link Ben Manso to the boy's disappearance, Gomez dropped his investigation, not even bothering to inform the Santa Barbara police, who had reached their own dead end, about his suspicions. Iris Wong missed the story about Bobby's abduction from the hospital. When, some time later, Wade showed up at her office without Ben, and she asked about him, Wade told her

Ben had gone home to Chicago to be with his family. She asked no further questions. Bobby Velez entered the statistics of missing children.

The letter, postmarked from San Francisco, arrived without a return address. Rios opened it and removed a single sheet of paper. Unfolding it, he read:

> *Tell Georgie we're fine. I'm working and Bobby's in school and doing well. Turns out, he's really smart. To our neighbors we're just father and son. I have a favor to ask you. There's an old man named Wade London who lived downstairs from me. Would you call him and tell him we're okay? I know he's been worried. You won't hear from me again, so thank you.*

There was no signature. Rios wrote down the name Wade London, then torn the letter into indecipherable pieces and scattered them in the trash. He buzzed his secretary.

"Arjay, see if you can find me a phone number for a Wade London in West Hollywood."

A moment later she buzzed him back with the information. Rios picked up the phone and dialed.

About Michael Nava

Michael Nava is the six-time Lambda Literary award-winning author of the Henry Rios novels and the historical novel, *The City of Palaces* (University of Wisconsin Press, 2014). His most recent work, *Lay Your Sleeping Head* (Kórima Press, 2016), a reimaagining of the first Henry Rios novel, was hailed as "one of the literary events of the year," and earned him his tenth Lambda Literary award nomination. You can find him on fb.com/MichaelNavaWriter or www.michaelnavawriter.com.

Made in the USA
Columbia, SC
06 November 2018